MOUNTAIN(R)

MOUNTAIN  R

Jacques Jouet
TRANSLATION BY BRIAN EVENSON

DALKEY ARCHIVE PRESS

First published in France by Éditions du Seuil, 1996
Copyright © 1996 by Jacques Jouet
Translation copyright © 2004 by Brian Evenson

First English edition, 2004

Library of Congress Cataloging-in-Publication Data

    Jouet, Jacques, 1947-
      [Montagne R. English]
      Mountain R / by Jacques Jouet ; translated by Brian Evenson. — 1st Dalkey
Archive ed.
        p. cm.
      ISBN 1-56478-330-8 (alk. paper)
       I. Evenson, Brian, 1966- II. Title.

PQ2670.O926M6613 2004
843'.914—dc22

                            2003055443

Partially funded by grants from the Illinois Arts Council, a state agency
and the French Ministry of Culture.

Dalkey Archive books are published by the Center for Book Culture, a nonprofit organization,
located at Milner Library, Illinois State University

www.centerforbookculture.org

Printed on permanent / durable acid-free paper and bound in the United States of America.

Table of Contents

I - The Speech
1

II - The Construction Site
25

III - The Trial (short excerpt)
95

I

<u>The Speech</u>

Speaker of the House — The floor belongs to the president of the Republican Council.

The president of the Republican Council — We must do something. We must. Something must be done, something must be accomplished. It must not be said that we have not done anything. We must do more, and do it better than anyone has ever done. And moreover, this extraordinary something, we *will* do it. We have already conceived it, and are here to make it official. This something even has a name, and its name is *The Mountain . . . Republic Mountain . . .* it is *Mountain R!* Now *there's* a name that says it all. Mountain with a capital *R*. We shall call it henceforth *Mountain R*. The Republic is magnificent—long live the Republic!—but it looks like a flat-chested girl. Too bad! But we are going to alter her, the Republic . . . we are here to act . . . to give her what we can: a womanly figure. The most beautiful girl in the world can afford to give all she has and more, if that beautiful girl is the Republic . . . the Republic of exceptional self-improvement! Is there anything more beautiful than a mountain? Anything healthier? We shall build a mountain. Among us let it be said, we

are agreed! The meeting is adjourned. *(Noise.)* Of course
not . . . I'm joking! The meeting has clearly just started!
So . . . what do you have to say about my idea? We will build
a mountain in the open air. Who is opposed? Calm down
. . . obviously, you won't vote yet! I've hardly begun to extol
Mountain R for you, and, I warn you, I will not be brief, but
rather, exhaustive. You know . . . no, you can't know, but
you must come to know . . . I'll tell you a secret . . . When
I was a little boy—I hear you saying: "That wasn't yesterday!"—born on the working-class slopes of Petit-Montluc
(that's a secret from nobody), my grandmother used to say,
poor woman, born there long before me, that she would
cut off the ears (and she was being polite!) of the official
who would level the slope or alter even the slightest part
of the Basilica of the Precious-Blood (although she hated
the priest and was not a good Catholic). I intend not to dis-
appoint her, or, better stated, pull the rug out from under
her poor dead feet. Action must be taken. We have been
elected for that and we are not going to fail. It is true that
we have been slightly delayed because we had to bring some
order to the disastrous situation we were handed: this failed
Republican (if it still merits that lovely adjective) budget in
which debt has put more holes than a piece of Swiss cheese!
(Applause from the right.) Now is the time. The Republic is
sick with ninety diseases. Not one fewer. Perhaps more. To
cut to the chase, let's say ninety-two. Ninety proven, two

more for good measure . . . We've counted them. I'm not going to read you a list. This isn't the place for it. You hate lists, and so do I. And then, you know these diseases all too well: you either fought them *(the speaker indicates the seats to the right)* or encouraged them to grow *(the speaker indicates the seats to the left)* . . . What do you think? Are we not short on time? Besides, a committee is ceaselessly working, at least I hope so . . . let's wisely await its conclusions. Good. But let us not wait before acting and building. From this moment on, we can begin to sort out this mess we've created. The Republic is sick with three deadly diseases, and obviously a great many minor illnesses. There are the first two, upon which I won't dwell: old age and eternal childishness . . . and finally the third: the great need for a far-reaching enterprise, for a spirited and mobilizing enterprise. The Republic is a stalled ship. It's up to us to put wind in her sails! *(The speaker waits for applause that does not come.)* Therefore we've thought of this great notion of a grand mountain (which is no less a grand notion of a great mountain), which will provide members of the Republic with good air for the lungs, the fragrance of high-country pines, snow for the eye to admire, peace and quiet for our children, and skiing for all! Picture if you please the Republic, already visited by tourists, when by satellite and by word of mouth it will cry out to its potential visitors, waiting at the four corners of the world, that we are the Republic of

Mountain R! Do you doubt that this endeavor, so simple, this idea, so timely, will not attract the most jaded tourist, and even be exportable for sale throughout the wide and wonderful world? Can you imagine that countries as flat as Holland, as monotonous as Mongolia, to give only two examples, won't declare themselves willing, the very next day, to acquire a ready-to-use mountain, after visiting our prototype? A sister mountain, daughter of our clever Republican know-how ... Remember ... Before we took charge of the Republic, they accused us of preparing to liquidate the Republican idea.

Mr Carmicael— Certainly! Further, those who said it ...

From the right and the center — Don't interrupt!

The president of the Republican Council — Oh, but you can very well let this gentleman speak! He doesn't bother me at all. His song, I know it by heart, this bird! Remember a time when you dared to say, Mr Carmicael, that tomorrow, if we were elected, the word *Republic* itself would be placed under glass in the Museum of National Memory? I call upon your sense of honesty to acknowledge officially that we did not begin this new millennium by trampling upon the Republic. Everyone saw this—with their own eyes!—and their mouths should not now betray them. The government will no longer be mismanaged. We have preserved the heritage of the Republic, the whole

Republic, and nothing but the Republic! What's more, we have added several original flourishes, among which not the least is the courageous law on Shared Rights. *(Hissing from the left.)* Thank you, gentlemen. I see that you are still alive and breathing. I see your health is good. That's because you indulge yourselves in certain privileges of the wealthy: daily hydrotherapy (100 percent reimbursed), or else your mountain chalet, far away, which you take off for whenever you feel like it, with a little dip of the wing of your private jet, with your little family . . . *(Uproar.)*

SPEAKER OF THE HOUSE — Gentlemen! I beg you . . . Let the president of the Republican Council speak.

THE PRESIDENT OF THE REPUBLICAN COUNCIL — But us, we think of all the others: of those who still take the train, when they can afford it, second class naturally, or those who know about snow only from television, particularly when the reception is bad. *(Murmurs and attempts to interrupt.)* Silence, now! We must move forward. How will we proceed? Quickly, and along legal channels. Public utility investigations and feasibility studies shall be conducted simultaneously. From this moment on . . .

MR CARMICAEL — Why isn't the Minister of Public Works at this meeting?

THE PRESIDENT OF THE REPUBLICAN COUNCIL — Because he's been detained! But there is only one government of the Republic, and, as you well know, Mr Carmicael, I will answer all of your questions! The file . . . of course I know the file! At this time, we declare an open competition for all architects of the Republic, the guidelines of which will appear in next month's *Official News*. Again, only for the nation's architects! Henceforth, topographical, geotechnical, economic, and environmental studies are launched. All at once! The preliminary ground and site investigation . . . It appears altogether reasonable to imagine construction starting this coming spring, and to anticipate a project length of three or four years. I can already see the ballet of steam shovels and dump trucks, of steam rollers and other compactors, marching along the flanks of Mountain R . . . Is it not obvious that, by creating new jobs for the impoverished sector of the population, we are on the way to scoring a little victorious revolution against exclusionism, which is a chancre growing in our worldwide civilization, a civilization in which the Republic is not, moreover, the worst place to live? *("Yes, yes!" from the right.)* Here and there, obviously, the merits of our decision will be challenged . . . *(The speaker indicates the left.)* Unless your vehemence will give way in the face of huge social benefits, among which number thousands of newly created jobs, permanent and temporary? Oh, I know! . . . Objections will be raised from all sides . . . They're pre-packaged and always the same, they've been dragged along forever in the wastewater of all the world's gutters, where the opposition regularly causes itself to barely get wet. *(Voices from the left.)* I said *wet,* not *upset!* The opposition is unfortunately incapable of causing an *upset!*

MR CARMICAEL — I object! You deceive the Republic!

THE PRESIDENT OF THE REPUBLICAN COUNCIL — Mr Carmicael . . . this is unworthy of you. However, I was awaiting your riposte, and you know how I love a duel. Very well, *en garde!* I, too, object . . . because, believe it or not, I too am proud to have at one time been a member of the opposition . . . the only difference being that universal suffrage . . . *(interruption from the left)* . . . UNIVERSAL, I rightly said *universal,* the law which this assembly passed at the end of the last session is in no way a step backward for democracy. Without it, you would not be here. One voice a piece for each of the poorest families is real and demonstrable progress. We are not about to start that debate again, which already took up three long days. Let's get back to our great project! *(Clacking of desks, movement, and applause.)* Mr Speaker, perched like an eagle above this scrum of squeaking rats, I order you to use your gavel so that I can continue, or else have the room cleared . . . otherwise I must question the value of your leadership . . . Thank you, thank you . . . I was saying, then, that up there, on the slopes of our Mountain R, snowbound in winter and verdant in summer, the health of all citizens, like that of the Republic, as we have concieved it, will be fully restored. As often as possible, the concept over which . . . or rather . . . the *council* over which I preside will hold its meetings at the summit in a building that more befits our stature! We will all be energized by the multiplication of red blood cells, and thus the multiplication of ideas, and thus the multiplication of advanced and eminently exportable technologies! The competitiveness lost by generations of political maneuverers who today are grumbling is to be reignited from the spark of Mountain R. *(Inaudible objection from the center.)* Mr Bouton, you are one of the most respected of our parliamentarians. I thank you for that objection which is as measured as you are yourself. We'd thought of that. One of today's most eminent climatologists, Professor Kash-Ney of the University of Tirana, has promised, starting next month, to join the commission of specialists who will meet the designated architects, the engineers, the mountain climbers, the syndicate of owners-of-hotels-in-mountainous-surroundings, an ex-shepherd knows how to manage the seasonal movements of livestock, people capable of draining water, underground specialists (soil mechanics, geodynamics . . .) and those snowblowing hellions, etc., etc. *(Laughter from among all seats.)*

Mr Carmicael — Such an imagination!

The president of the Republican Council — Let it be written, here, let it be remembered, that the laughter that comes from the seats to the left makes me sick at heart. Blah! I'd vomit my breakfast onto the lectern if I were not in an honorable assembly. This laughter emanates from cold hearts that cannot picture the poor citizens of the eastern quarters, bareheaded all winter, bent over a bad fire whose fumes poison them, thin, torn up, languishing, without shirts on their backs or shoes on their feet, more like men dragged out of the pit than the living, who, lifting their hands to you again, as if to the image of God, trying to make up their minds whether to hurl at you the arrows or bombs of fortune so as to constrain you to a more just redistribution of wealth, entreat you with these words you don't want to hear which I now interpret for you, since your deafness won't listen: "How long shall it be, gentlemen, before the wounds with which we are afflicted shall be acknowledged? How long shall it be that bad advice will make members of parliament believe they can boundlessly and endlessly kill, against the traditions and laws of this country, those unrecognized by the world, already disenfranchised, without ever taking the opinion of those persons into account? How much flattery must be paid to our representatives before they will consider that they have not obeyed the laws or observed the smallest moral contracts with their voters?" He who acts like an ostrich, with his head in the sand, continues to laugh, like Mr Carmicael and his henchmen do, and will not be bothered by the sight of the wretches of this quite difficult century—the self-satisfied

11

heir of the previous one—who are now just dirty faces seated in the back rows, a hundred leagues away from your good favor, clumsy, illiterate, with stinking feet, more like men devoted to nothingness than to suffering, aware only of their inability to disturb the pleasant unfolding of your princely lives, they being too occupied with the twists and turns of poverty and epidemics. *(Yawns from center left.)* You will nevertheless allow me to interpret for your plugged ears the shrieks that come to mar your self-importance and your fine appearance: "The time has come when we will no longer accept the injuries afflicted upon us in your care. From now on we have, in the highest levels of power, hearts that hear us . . ."

A VOICE — Hearts with little ears!

THE PRESIDENT OF THE REPUBLICAN COUNCIL — ". . . Never again shall we be served the leftovers of pain and bitterness, nor will we look more like men to be tossed into the pit than men to be greeted! Will it again be necessary for us to march on the boulevard chanting slogans? We will march!"

MR CARMICAEL — We shall meet in the street!

MR MOUTHE *(to Mr Carmicael)* — The street doesn't belong to you!

THE PRESIDENT OF THE REPUBLICAN COUNCIL — Thank you, gentlemen. You have the right to speak and you have spoken. Thus, you have justified the law of free speech, and, by that, the very observance of law. In speaking, you are abiding by and advocating for the law. Thank you. Now be lawmakers! Mountain R is at the heart of it. It's already there in our fierce determination, standing like the dried marshes of Pontains, the hillocks of the Zuydersee conquered across the Atlantic, the iron roadway of the Rouzat aqueduct, the waters of the canal-bridge at Briare, the tunnel under La Mancha or the doubly grand work of Ferdinand de Lesseps . . .

Mr Carmicael — Sit down and send out the checks!

The president of the Republican Council — Oh, certainly not, we won't need to bribe anyone! You on the left are wrong! As usual! We don't employ those corrupt practices which you yourselves used so well while you were in power! Not a single person, not even a fox or a crow (as in the fable), will find in this affair the least bit of cheese, for we are going to launch an immense public fundraising campaign that will finance the first portion of the construction! And the private investors will follow as if a single man! People will say: "You leave up to the public's generosity a project which taxes would usually pay for . . ." Two-century-old logic! Poor worn-out notion, ready to be put in the Museum of Failures and Atrocities. (*"Very good!" from the right.*) Mountain R shall be built. It is our will. It is will plain and simple, hardening the wills of all. It is cement. And don't believe that we've won in advance! Our dear neighbors will surely not let us work in peace. They'll come sniff at our Mountain; they'll come spy on it, try to sabotage it . . . We'll welcome them as is right and proper. Nobody will be without a job, because Mountain R is unitary, and therefore *unifying.* The higher it is, the more important the citizen will feel from having given tangible form to that which towers over him. It will be, for the exemplary Republic, the metaphysics of this brand-new century, a century which will be metaphysical or else nothing much at all. Mountain R! Mountain R! You already fill our days and nights. Who still has days to waste? And who has nights? Days and nights for the Republic of great undertakings? Whatever side you're on, you who like the mountains as well as you who prefer the sea, you workers of the fields, the sublime dung-daubed, you, deep-rooted townsfolk, or you with coal-darkened faces and with ankles chained together, rejoin the lifeline of Mountain R! *(Copious applause from the right and from the center.)* Thank you . . . thank you on her behalf . . . the Republic, gentlemen . . .

MADAME WALSA — There are also *ladies* in the assembly! *(Laughter.)*

THE PRESIDENT OF THE REPUBLICAN COUNCIL — The Republic, ladies . . . *(Laughter.)* I'm not stingy, and I like women, I'm not afraid to say it, I like women, even in the House . . . Now the Republic, our lady, is she a maritime power? Hardly. Is she still an agricultural power? There

14

are no longer agricultural powers, nowhere in the world! Why doesn't she become an original power, a mountainous power? Think it over for five minutes . . . Otherwise the Republic will end up cursed with a *lessened* power that will stick to her as unpleasantly as a plastic shower curtain! *(Groans from the left.)* The Republic is Alpine, Pyrenean, Massif-Centralian, Jurassian, Vosgean, Ardenais, Arian, Cevenoloean, Montlucian and Morvandian . . . I'm skipping some of them, the most beautiful . . . Our mountain must be sacred for us, an inheritance from the past and a reserve for the future. Should the Republic's government function just day to day, always in waiting, desperate to make ends meet? Shouldn't it contemplate from a bit higher up (we wish for a minimum of 1500 meters) the future of the generations that are its reponsibility, the future of this grand democracy . . . *(someone in the public gallery starts agitating)* . . . certainly, sir! exactly! . . . labor-intensive, industrial, commercial, po-e-tic! entrusted to it?

MR CARMICAEL — 1500 meters! but you will be in the clouds! You already are . . .

MR SCHLUTH — Like Hitler at Berchtesgaden!

THE PRESIDENT OF THE REPUBLICAN COUNCIL — Gentleman . . . please control yourselves! Don't forget who you are . . . of what body . . . Do not forget to whom you speak, nor in what name! Since we have ruled with a firm hand, our government has been insulted in every way possible! They

15

have called us not only clumsy, but also criminal, aggressive, crooked . . . Didn't they go so far as to call us clerics? That one, that's the best! *(Various movements.)* Of all these reproaches, gentlemen, only one affects me . . .

Mr Nourdine — Your politics are closed-door politics!

The president of the Republican Council — . . . and that's it! Closed-door! This is truly the most unlikely of reproaches! When everything is deliberated, in this very place, day after day! When the duration of parliamentary sessions has been more than doubled! When the number of members of parliament was increased at the time of the parliamentary division that followed the dissolution! When we have never been less shaken by events! Haven't we left Europe without difficulty and with our heads high? *(Shuffling from the left.)* It seems on that score that it is considered bad for a government to manifest ambition! Obviously, that contradicts the recent past! Unfortunately, gentlemen, you'll have no choice but to swallow this ambition, choke on it, if need be. Take a look at those hard-working nations around you, which have fasted so long . . . Look at those who nibble away at the paltry lead that we've failed to increase . . . look at those who shall soon overtake us and who no longer call any effort impossible! Look at those who build their economies on traditional products. Up to us to pick up the gauntlet and innovate!

Or else, let's go to sleep! Let's empty our cellars, get our women and children drunk, squeeze them tight, stick our heads under our wings, and sleep. And then what? A mountain! We must think it over! No one has thought of it, no one but us! Here lies, gentlemen, the true meaning of our endeavor . . . here we have, let me tell you, a goal far loftier than your niggling questions of wallet and purse . . . "Anti-Republican," is that what our Mountain R is, as suggested in some newspaper or other? Would you let your mother's body die from lack of a healthy kidney? Let he who would do so die first from his own cold-heartedness! No, gentlemen, no, ladies, there is not one among you here, not one, who would not submit to a life-saving transplant in order to prolong his mother's life. *("Nicely put!" on many sides.)* The year after my coming to power, conducting with full sincerity an examination of my conscience . . . *(interruptions and ironic laughter from the center right and the extreme left which provoke objections from the center left and right)* . . . I tell you that I consider the reproach of being imprudent as the most non-merited . . .

Mr Lecorre — Use proper grammar!

The president of the Republican Council — . . . the most non-merited of criticisms (idiot!) that might be applied to us! A government that is always juggling two obligations—to make the most of its resources and its public image—will always arrive at the simplistic conclusion of inaction and immobility. A good government knows how to wait, to seem timorous: it is the tension in the bow. It is taking aim. But the arrow has left the quiver! The bow is drawn. A good government does not fear to release the bowstring, because it knows that the arrow cannot miss the bull's-eye if perseverence has been sufficiently great! And what today is the bull's-eye? To stop emphatically the influx of immigrants! But not to stop them by force or by expulsion. We must put an end to this infernal logic of idle government! We must create an army of workers composed of those among our nationals who are left out in the cold, and we must rent this army to our clients as soon as it has won its first battle. So, we will help put together local brigades who will no longer just daydream of getting work or of loafing around in our country. Ha ha! What a beautiful ambition! Far loftier needs oblige us. Far be it from us to gripe about this obligation. It is its own reward! I think today of our mourned colleague Julius Watzki . . .

MADAME BRUN — Ah no, not him! Let him rest in peace! Do you hear me? There are limits to what you will be allowed to denigrate!

THE PRESIDENT OF THE REPUBLICAN COUNCIL — I don't believe, Madame Brun, who is interrupting me, that what I am going to say about Julius Watzki could destroy his memory. At the very most it would curtail the moving, though questionable, manner in which you and your friends try to appropriate that memory—a memory of a man who, in his own time, never wanted to sentimentalize the past. The past doesn't interest us. We surrender it to you with all our hearts. We are looking to bury the past through action! And let it be suffocated by action, unto a beautiful death! Let us remember Julius Watzki, the humble Julius Watzki who, it's true, advocated limited government and more power in the hands of the people! The catch is that, after all is said and done, the government must have the will to look the people in the eye. We are no longer afraid of taking risks and paying for them! Some rulers, believe it or not, some rulers are afraid of their people . . . the scoundrels! That's how you can recognize them. And I'd like in this regard to recount an anecdote to you. When two weeks ago I went with the Minister of the Distribution of Ever-Fewer-Jobs and Retraining Department to visit the city of Trente, at La Chapelle— that city which has had such bad press that no minister until ourselves, no subprefect, no private eye, had dared to go there—while we were drinking an Orangina in the youth center, near a Ping-Pong table with a tattered net, answering with the greatest possible frankness all the questions that were posed to us in front of the cameras of our television networks, whom in passing I thank . . . There was a young man there, half of whose face was so horribly deformed that his words were a bit garbled (the after-effects of childhood illnesses poorly treated). Holding what had once been a paddle in his hand, he sucked on a month-old stick from an ice-cream bar. I made my way toward him, without the least repulsion, and, feeling that it was my duty to take him into my trust so I might have a chance to hear the message he was burning to convey, I put an arm around his shoulders and put my ear to his lips in order to hear what was in his heart. And what was it in his heart? Well . . . nobody dreams of interrupting me now, it seems . . . he had a *wreck* in his heart. A ship worn down to its iron-work sinews, never used and yet eaten away with rust. Eighteen years old and with tons of the scrap iron of bitterness in his heart! And that I shall not forget. Nor his stammering of phrases which spit out like bullets from a machine gun . . . barely articulate . . . I said to him: "Come with me, we'll build a mountain." —"Get the fuck out!" —"I'll hire you."—"I don't believe you."—"You're mistaken."—"Can I be friends with you too?"—"Yes, why couldn't you be friends with me?"—"Because you're on TV every day!"—"You too, you'll be on television tomorrow. It depends entirely on you. Of course you can be friends with me!"—"You're screwing with me!"—"No, I'm not screwing with you, I'm hiring you. It's different. Are you deaf or what? There's a mountain to build!"—"What the hell are you talking about?"—"Mountain R."—"A real mountain?"—"More real than the real ones! The mountain of tomorrow . . . Republic Mountain."—"What's the Republic?"—"It's your second mother."—"Why make a mountain?"—"To occupy your time, to keep you busy."—"I don't want to be kept busy."—"Ha! You dream of nothing else!"—"Why would I believe you?"—"What else do you have to do?"—"Nothing."—"Why don't you fix the Ping-Pong net?"—"Woman's work."—"So?"—"What. . . ?"—"A mountain, in exchange for that!"—"All right, I'm coming."—"Leave your paddle, put your affairs in order."—"That's easily done."—"You'll sleep on bare ground."—"I'll sleep."—"Well done!"—"Can my buddy come too?"—"Is he strong?"—"Like Rambo."—"Your buddy can come, too." *(Murmurs.)* At this moment, they're working. They're taking lessons to get their heavy equipment licenses. They'll drive the first dump truck. Mountain R will begin its ascent at 40 kilometers east of the capitol. Even from here, in clear weather, we'll see the summit. From the summit, visitors will watch through binoculars the House where the daily fate of the Republic is discussed. The chosen site is the best possible, taking into consideration all the parameters. We will of course give just compensation to those few landowners who live on the grounds honored by history to host the foundation of

Mountain R. A few villages will be buried, as happened before, when hydroelectric dams had to be built. We can surely deal with these issues. Those inhabitants, particularly dear to our hearts, won't have *us* to complain about. State emergency. No emergency more of an emergency than *that* emergency! It's what we're going to do, and it will be our greatest accomplishment! Our claim to history shall be this thing we've done, because it will have been done, and because nobody but us will have done it. The mountain will give birth to us. Sons of Mountain R. Mountain R, daughter of the Republic, and conversely, the Republic as daughter of Mountain R. The mother, daughter of her daughter. The daughter, daughter of her mother. Because it can only be done with the voices that are assembled here to do something that not one among us could do alone. Thus, we say: Mountain R! A bit of the good old real, against all that is virtual! Sing Mountain R! Raise yourselves to its height! Breathe at last the intoxicating resin of its conifers! You already look better! O Mountain, rise and rise further! Build level upon level upon level! And the woodpecker on the ridgepole! Look, snow, the first snowfall! The first snowfall on the bare mountain! And look, edelweiss! Look, snowplows and gentian, mountain streams, trout. Look, shepherds' paths, springs, sheep . . . beehives . . . beehives everywhere and honey for all! To each according to his desires! To each according to his means! Hello, magnificent countryside! We have entered the age of *Mountain R!*

   (The submitted text is adopted without amendments.)

II

<u>The Construction Site</u>

—It won't bother you to answer?

—Oh, not at all, why would it bother me?

—I don't know.

—Go ahead, go right ahead, young lady. It gives me such pleasure that you've found a career! I always knew that you'd get there. You're doing a lot better, eh?

—I'm happy that you're happy.

—Then everybody's happy.

—In fact, I'm not very sure of having found a "career," as you say, but perhaps that's finally changing . . . and besides, that's not the issue today . . .

—You try, at least . . . If your mother were still here, she'd have smiled her nice smile, seeing you like this. But . . . you have nothing to tape record with?

—No, I don't much like working with a tape recorder. Going over the tapes is too boring, and then I don't pay close attention. You tell yourself: It's no big deal if I miss something, there's the tape . . . so you fall asleep . . . No, I prefer to take notes, if it's really necessary. But as you can see, I don't even have a notepad. I have a good memory, though. At school, my teachers always told me that I had a phenomenal memory. It's true, I think.

27

—I've pointed it out too, you know . . . Well, let's get started.

— . . .

—Well?

—Here goes. So, my dear father, who has been retired for three years and who isn't the least bit bored, you are going to tell me what you think of the construction project, which now seems to be treading water a little, right?

—Yes, apparently. That was bound to happen, but it's rather sad! I never understood much about finance, you know . . . If you rely on me for . . . a thing of that magnitude, it only makes sense that there might be some overruns. From there, to truly knowing the ins and outs . . .

—Wait, don't go so fast . . . You yourself started when?

—The mountain? I started . . . it isn't hard to remember, you were fourteen years old. I remember perfectly the day you turned fourteen. It was the day after the day the deal was struck. It was so tremendous . . . Do you remember?

—Yes. I remember the meal. It was a meal for rich people. A meal that was a little bit sad. I remember my three dresses, and some earrings.

—I see that you still wear those earrings under your pretty hair . . . Just for today or . . . ?

—Nearly every day since that time!

—Is that right? Well, that's what I call a present! And the dresses?

—Dresses don't last as long!

—That's for sure.

—Yes. So . . . the contract, how did you get it?

—Ah, it's very complicated . . .

—Hmm, we'll get to the heart of the matter . . .

—If you want.

—Go ahead.

—First I should talk about my beginnings, because, it's true, I've never told you about all that . . . but there's no reason to be ashamed, eh . . .

—Of course not. Why would you be?

—You must not remember much about your grandfather . . .

—A little bit, maybe.

—He was quite a character, my father! He considered himself to be the prototype of the Italian immigrant mason, a rough-drawn caricature . . . He made a great effort to try to preserve all the signs of his ethnic origins: the broad-backed silhouette, the tousled hair, the rugged accent that never changed from the day he figured that he could understand everything in French and have everything understood . . . He spoke so badly! But he was a man of extraordinary courage. He wanted me to get an education. He wanted me to study, and the subject that obsessed him was history. He told me: "There is one unforgiveable thing for a man who dies at war: not to know why he

29

died. If—God forbid!—that should happen to you, son, make sure you know why!" When I was ten years old, he built an office for me at our house, on the flat roof of the apartment, without a construction permit . . . with heating! I was more than a little proud! I had books, a slide rule, even a typewriter! That was how I was able to get as far as technical college, after which I fooled around a bit with some artists . . . I wasted my time, and that hurt him. Back then I thought only about having fun; I did scenery and management for a theater troupe. We were very impressed with ourselves . . . We believed in what we were doing . . . yet, how awful we were! And annoying! What wasted energy . . .

—No, don't say that!

—I wasn't the type to stick with it. It didn't please him one bit, the old man . . . didn't understand . . . but he forgave me when I took up masonry. He helped me. He gave me my first truck, not completely new but in good shape . . . it didn't have any dents or scratches . . . Meanwhile, he was losing his eyesight. He couldn't drive anymore. Then his plumb line ran out, so to speak.

—How did your business grow?

—That resulted from the economic situation, you know . . . the '70s were still prosperous, the '80s were hard, the '90s as well: building was slack. You tightened your belt, you juggled, always trying not to go bankrupt. I succeeded.

You coddled the vehicles, so that they'd last, so that you wouldn't have to get new ones. Hauling, dumping, digging . . . your mother went into accounting . . . and it was generous on her part, because personally she was more into design . . . she designed glasses, the frames of glasses . . . and she could have been successful! People said she had imagination. I was the one who should have learned accounting . . . But it's true that the Mountain made us take off like an arrow, almost too rapidly. It was madness, I see that now, but okay, I was no longer a kid, and I felt it was the last big chance of my professional life. It tempted me, so I threw myself in like my life depended on it.

—That, I remember.

—I did notice that you suffered from it a little, but I'm going to tell you one thing: I thought about you every day, all the time I was off trying to find filler for the mountain. There's no way for you to have known . . . That paid for your fancy schooling in Switzerland. At least you don't blame me anymore . . .

—Papa, I would really prefer not to talk about that. I'm not questioning you about the family, you know, but about the construction site.

—Yes, yes. Anyway, it's more interesting.

—Today, yes. So, what else?

—Not much . . . next, work. Work, that's all . . . We had to build a mountain, not sit around thinking . . . The

funniest thing is that I already had a little experience . . .
I'd had a client in the '80s who'd watched as an arm of the
freeway was constructed through the far end of his country house's garden. He'd gone half-crazy with rage, and
without any authorization he'd started building a sort of
mountainette, a wall against the noise . . . 500 meters long,
at least! He'd started it all alone, and then ended up hiring
me, me and my truck, to help him finish. It was the same
kind of work . . . day after day after day after day. What
was hard with Mountain R was that the business had to
get bigger, you see? . . . I mean our business . . . so, in the
first stage that only increased the load, the red tape . . .
It's terribly complicated . . . You have to have just the right
number of workers. You have to be well advised. I had a
good accountant, thank God. But still, your mother had
an enormous weight on her shoulders, and at times she
didn't feel like she had enough schooling, so we had to
build up her confidence . . . she had to teach herself . . .
Sometimes the pressure was too much for her . . . That's
how it was, though, what can you do? . . . There wasn't
a choice.

—Papa, you don't have to justify yourself. I'm not here
to criticize your choices. Nobody is responsible for mother's
cancer, not you or anyone else . . . What interests me is having
the details about the construction site. Maybe it's stupid of
me, but I was under the impression that the site was a State

within the State . . . very complicated . . . The daily life of the Republic during the time of the construction of Mountain R . . . that's my subject. It has nothing to do with your little secrets . . .

—Why are they interested in that, these Americans of yours?

—Who knows?

—Well . . . everyday life . . . yes, nothing extraordinary happened, exactly, it was everyday . . .

—You're not trying very hard!

—You're funny . . . Ask me some questions, perhaps that will be easier.

—Okay, for example, what time did you wake up in the morning?

—4 AM.

—All the time?

—Oh, yes . . . still do!

— But you didn't sleep at home.

—That depended. There were many phases. The first two years, I drove a truck. Later, I spent most of my time at the office, but that didn't suit me, I wanted something more hands-on. Later, I started driving again . . . But I moved around a lot. I never slept at the construction site. The Company had . . .

—The Mountain R Company?

—Yes, the MRC, the Company had—you know this—

33

cut the pie in half . . . well, two very unequal halves. Bargeco officially had the whole contract (in fact, he'd had to enter into partnership with another huge company, but smaller than his), but the contract required that he also use small businesses. It was politics, right, it's obvious, because from the point of view of the efficiency of the job, it was a lot of wasted energy, see . . . it multiplied the number of cogs . . . Having said that, it was Bargeco who ran the whole thing, a sort of commander-in-chief so to speak . . . So, one had, we had, a share of the deal. It was unexpected.

—A share of the deal, just like that?

—Yes, yes. Your mother was so happy when we got it! It came at a very tough time. We could no longer make ends meet, and were about to go live in the country.

—Oh, there's even less work in the country!

—Yes, but there's land and time to grow vegetables. And all the space that was needed for the design board . . . the frames of glasses . . . We seriously considered it. And then, this other thing happened.

—You had confidence?

—Confidence in what? Above all we had confidence in ourselves, yes to that. The prime of life . . . even if for me it seemed already a bit late, but I still felt young . . . and, you see, she was the first of us to go . . . Shit!

—What?

—This shitty life . . .

—No, I meant to say, did you have faith in . . . in the government . . . in the Mountain?

—Me? I'll tell you, it all struck me as a bit crazy sometimes, late at night . . . When the day's work had worn me out . . . but especially in the morning, when it takes everything you have to get going. Your mother teased me about it, but I know she thought the same thing. She forced herself to have faith. Somehow or other, we helped each other. On my own, I know it wouldn't have worked.

—How did you hear about it?

—On the evening news, like everybody else.

—The news of the project, but what about the invitation for bids?

—Ah, that was through Di Pascale, from the Union.

—Who's he?

—Di Pascale . . . you don't remember him?

—No . . .

—And yet he used to sit you on his knee. He used to visit us, once upon a time . . . At the Trône carnival he paid for you to play that game where you toss the cloth ball at the cardboard heads . . . You didn't hit a single head, so he told you to imagine that one of them was your mother's, and you got it on the first try!

—Oh, that was him! That was naughty! In fact, I don't remember, but I've been told about it so often! Di Pascale . . . I'd forgotten the name.

—Di Pascale was quite a character.

—Did he have a company too?

—Yes, like me . . . a little bit bigger . . . well, three or four times bigger . . . Damn old Di Pascale . . .

—Is he still there?

—Where?

—At the construction site?

—No. Well, yes, in a certain way. He stayed there. He's dead. He died in his truck. You could say that he fell off Mountain R. He plummeted with his truck. The place was a filthy mess.

—Isn't it still?

—Oh, I don't want to know what it is now.

—Do you have any idea how many deaths there've been?

—The usual number, you know . . . Public works have always been like that. Nothing can be done about it.

—And there weren't more than usual?

—That's not my impression.

—You're serious?

—Of course!

—Then how did it happen?

—For Di Pascale? Well, it's very simple . . . to climb to the summit, or I should say the provisional summit, to the summit that was a little bit higher each day . . . but not a lot higher . . . they made a more or less packed down road . . .

there were many of these . . . normally, the road systems were for heavy trucks, I purposefully said *normally* . . . And then a portion of the road collapsed, a stupid accident, and then undoubtedly he was overloaded . . .

—You were still there?

—No. Well, yes . . . I'd retired, but was having difficulty staying at home. Your mother had just died. So, from time to time, I went to give Di Pascale a hand. It kept me busy. I had experience. It was two years ago, yes, about two years ago . . .

—And you were there the day . . .

—What?

—The day of Di Pascale's accident . . .

—Yes.

—It hurts you to talk about it . . . We can talk about it some other time.

—No, no.

—In the press there's nothing about these accidents. The journalists complain that they weren't allowed to do their work. Is it true that the construction site was restricted?

—Nobody could enter unless Bargeco approved, Bargeco's watchmen . . . very well supported, very well armed . . . They weren't fooling around, Bargeco's watchmen. God!

—And Di Pascale was the only one to die that day?

—Yes, yes. He was driving all alone.

—You're sure?

—In the back of his truck he had a huge pile of glass. He was too overloaded. I'd told him so. Glass is very heavy . . . 2.6 tons per cubic meter . . . whereas potatoes, only 750 kilograms per cubic meter . . .

—Why glass?

—You know, one of the great problems in public works is the balancing of excavated material and filler. The more it balances out, the less time it takes and the less expensive it is! At Mountain R, you weren't pampered! The hard thing about that bitch of a mountain was to find material, filler, without having to dig a hole to get dirt. What would we have done with such holes?

—You could've made a lake at the foot of the mountain!

—Yes . . . as a matter of fact that had been one of the projects considered, but I don't really know, it didn't mesh with geological conditions . . . Because those had to be considered . . . They took into account the number of cubic meters needed to . . .

—But the glass?

—The glass made up part of the scrap that was supplied to us. Anything was good, demolitions, quarry waste, industrial waste, household garbage . . . There were endless discussions among the engineers to figure out if anything was going to be more or less stable . . . They quickly gave up on household waste, because it decomposed . . . So, that's when they started to use glass . . .

—A glass mountain . . .

—Yes . . . well, it didn't make it transparent . . . And at any rate they didn't use much glass. They used it only during the six months when recycling glass was in vogue. You could salvage it dirt cheap . . . Later, there was the requisition of the northern slag heaps, those to the east, where there was still potash in the last century . . . But the inhabitants there were used to their little mountains . . . I remember a slag heap near Lens . . . to salvage it, you worked under the protection of the riot police . . . There were demonstrations everywhere, old people, associations, students from the schools . . . Can you picture it? What a mess! But okay, in all the great construction projects of the world there are always problems like that, eh? It wasn't as exceptional as you might think . . . Look, here's what I can tell you about the construction site. I'm glad to be free of it, you know . . . After a while, I had nightmares. I, who'd never been afraid of heights, my legs started to tremble when I got out of the truck. After Di Pascale's accident, I stopped for good. I had better things to do. Since then, all is well. So, now, let's have something to drink. That should be enough information for you, right?

—Yes to something to drink and yes to a break . . . but

that's really not enough information for me. No, no alcohol for me. Well, okay, sure! Wait . . . give me a beer.

—This is a good one. Me too, I'll start with beer. And then later we'll go have lunch.

—Yes.

—Aaah . . .

—It's good.

—It's Belgian . . . Those Belgians are quite ingenious when it comes to beer.

—Well . . . What did you drink when you were driving your truck?

—Beer, of course . . . not beer as strong as this here . . . no, beer bought by the liter, two or three percent, practically rainwater . . . and only for the sake of quenching my thirst.

—When I see big public works projects like that . . . such as a freeway . . . and I see men working every day, making a little progress every day . . . I try to imagine how that must be to . . . their relation to time . . . the daily advance of a few meters . . . the patience . . . It must take extraordinarily patience.

—Yes, but a construction project, you know, when you work on it, it's not what the public sees. If it were, it would be boring. No, the finished project is an enormous quantity of little things, little tasks . . . some demand a week, others three days, others a morning, others a month and a half . . . You realize that the only thing you know is that you're involved in this business for several years of your life, and that during those years you won't do much else . . . not much beyond finishing an infinity of little tasks . . .

—Ants . . .

—Busy little beavers!

—Always the same scenery . . .

—Never the same scenery! And you're the one changing it.

—You and others . . . But it's imperceptible!

—Yes.

—It would have been worth the effort to take a picture every day of the same place . . .

—I believe that's been done.

—I'm sure . . . How many days altogether?

—Me? Oh . . . hundreds . . . no, thousands.

—And isn't that sad?

—No, it's *not* sad! First of all because you have a job, which isn't the case for everyone . . .

—Next?

—Because a person likes to be doing something . . . and something a little bit prestigious . . . There's no comparison . . . To be able to say that during all those years I took part in the construction of Mountain R, I can't help it, it's satisfying. Is that foolish?

—I didn't say so . . . I'm thinking . . . all things considered, building Versailles must have been a bit the same. The

Hundred Steps, for instance . . . what's that if not a Mountain R! . . . but *R* as in Royal, then. And there were two of them. Two times a hundred.

—I don't know.

—Papa . . .

—Yes?

—You had employees?

—Of course.

—When you started, how many employees did you have?

—In '67?

—No, at the beginning of the mountain . . .

—Because in '67, obviously, I was all alone, with my truck.

—Of course!

—'67 doesn't interest you very much, does it?

—No, not too much . . . not today.

—Well . . . at the beginning of the mountain? We were at the bare minimum. Let's see . . . your mother, me, two others at the busy times, one retiree from the railroad . . . he wasn't paid a lot but he had his retirement: a hard-working guy . . . two driver-in-training positions, handled by the State, and then, bit by bit, for a limited time, between two and five more . . . Yes, that's it.

—And the construction site changed that somehow?

—Of course.

—How?

—You took more risks . . . you speculated about the next day, it was unavoidable . . . And then the government blackmailed us when it came to hiring. It offered us . . . no, it *forced* on us its favorites. In fact, that's why I was on television. I had to hire this young guy who wasn't at all qualified, but he had friends in high places. Entirely by accident, no less, because the Council president stumbled onto him one day when he was making his tour of the soup kitchens. So, this kid, I tried to mold him. They foisted him on me, in front of the camera, like a newborn . . . Baptized him with the sweat of my brow! He meant well, but he was already a little bit handicapped . . . I didn't mention that . . . He'd passed his highway code, but I don't know how . . . no, I know how, the examiner received word from the Cabinet . . . I never made him drive a truck, it wasn't possible, but most of the time he came with me. He was useless. Little by little, he turned nasty. Apparently he'd believed the hype.

—And later?

—He disappeared. He had a buddy, they were two of a kind. But the other was a great hulking brute, and he joined the watchmen of the construction site.

—What was he called?

—The watchman?

—No, the other one.

—He was called Jean . . . Jean something . . . I've for-

43

gotten . . . They called him Jeannot.

—And you didn't keep a videotape? . . . of the broadcast?

—No. I didn't record it. I didn't have that kind of equipment.

—That's too bad.

—I didn't know what to say, I talked nonsense . . . You don't record yourself either . . . so you see . . .

—But apart from the people you were forced to hire, what about the others . . . ?

—Yes, we took . . . let's see . . . two months after the start of construction, we took first fifteen, then five others . . . one half were Turks, and the other Ukrainians. There were loads of them available. But they didn't last long. Jeannot couldn't stand Ukrainians, I don't know why . . . Later, we preferred retirees, because of their experience, or else the very young.

—And so he left, this Jean something?

—I never knew him well . . . I think he was killed in an accident . . .

—Him too?

—The Turks were the sort of workers you wanted . . .

—It's really incredible . . . those people from the government were elected on an anti-immigration platform, and you tell me that the crews were Turks and Armenians!

—Ukrainians.

—Right, Ukrainians.

—Yes, that's how it was, but the Republicans didn't take the brunt of it. We others were of the old school, Di Pascale, me . . . Lerebourg . . . Bensaïd . . . Célarier . . . very patient . . . no right to think about anything besides work. If you think about something besides work in this sort of thing, you quit at the end of two days, you don't even finish a week, and then you'll scrounge off your family, your union funds, or friends . . . you withdraw into your little cocoon, you don't care, you're at home. Foreigners don't have any of those options.

—But they were illegal workers.

—Yes and no. No, because we went out and got them, but it's true that their legal status was uncertain. They could be shipped back to their countries at any moment. In fact, that happened . . . a lot. It was stupid, they didn't have time to get trained . . . but those were Bargeco's methods.

—Where were they housed?

—How about we get some lunch?

—All right, I'm starting to get a bit hungry too. Beer on an empty stomach is a little rough.

—I could have offered you some olives. Ah! And I had a sausage . . .

—Too late. Let's go.

—What's the weather like outside? I haven't gone out yet today.

—Bring a coat.

—And my cap too. Let's go. The house seems big to me, now that your mother . . . So I often go out for lunch.

—You really look after the trees, don't you?

—Oh, I love my trees.

—But there aren't many flowers.

—The flowers were your mother's. You know . . . flowers aren't my speciality.

—To each his own. Why do you leave all that scrap metal there? It doesn't look very neat . . . and all those plastic things!

—Yes, I need to give them . . . A little while ago, you see, that would have been used for the mountain! Ha ha ha . . .

—This little pile?

—Oh, yes! No pile too small for Mountain R . . . ha ha ha . . .

—No, you, you stay there!

—We'll go on foot, that will give me a little exercise.

—Of course. We leave the dog, though, right?

—Yes, yes. Go that way. Just a couple of steps.

—He could have come with us, really.

—No, he's used to staying home.

—So, where did they live, the Turks and the Ukrainians? How many were there?

—There was a big city with cinder-block shanties and trailers, but comfortable enough . . . Naturally it was very controlled. They didn't want rogue huts springing up that would still be around after the construction project.

—Yes . . . that's what happened with the construction of Brasilia . . . the *favelas* . . . How many were there?

—That depended on the period . . . At the height of the construction project, several hundred, nearly a thousand.

—Nearly a thousand!

—Of course. It was a colossal piece of work, you know. It wasn't enough to dump the filler, it had to be processed, had to be packed tight . . . we had to avoid air pockets . . . it wasn't as mechanical as you might think. As for me, my boys were mostly drivers.

—The others were with Bargeco?

—The majority, yes!

—Where was it?

—What?

—The city . . .

—At the foot of the mountain . . . well, on one flank.

—Oh?

—Why are you surprised? . . . Go ahead. We'll sit over there. The sun is coming out a little. You'll see, this bistro . . . it's strange . . . if you happen to go to the restroom, the owner stops you on your way back . . . she gives you the bread to bring to table twelve . . . ha ha ha.

—That's sweet . . .

—What's today's special? . . . Hm . . . I like the rabbit,

but the pasta shells . . .

—Well, pasta suits me. I'm paying, okay, Papa? Yes, I insist, I got my advance . . . A carafe of Bordeaux. Did you go into their city yourself?

—No, but Jeannot did. He was buddies with the Turks. He didn't like the Ukrainians, but the Turks, yes. They had smorgasbords in their encampment on Saturday nights.

—Wait a minute, was it a city or an encampment?

—A city, yes. Should have said *city*.

—Should have said *city* or shouldn't have said anything?

—The Bargeco people told us to shut up about it, and that if we did we'd benefit. That suited me. It didn't cost me anything to keep quiet.

—Now that the construction project is on the verge of being halted, that no longer applies, you know.

—Yeah, yeah.

—Hmmm . . . Papa . . . in fact . . . it's not yet official, but it's stopped.

—The construction? Since when?

—Day before yesterday.

—How do you know that?

—I know. Does that bother you?

—I don't give a fuck.

—Jeannot, then, this Jeannot something . . . his death . . .

—Well?

— . . . that has nothing to do with the Turk encampment?

—Ah! the rabbit! Mmmm. It smells good. Thanks . . . Not the pasta shells, they're for my daughter. She works for Americans.

—You don't have to tell my life story . . .

—She's like a journalist . . .

—Not at all like a journalist, actually!

—Wait, there's something I didn't tell you . . . we're jumping around too much . . . The number of cubic meters, for a foundation three kilometers in diameter . . . a cone . . . you know how many cubic meters it takes?

—No idea.

—Three-and-a-half billion . . . Three-and-a-half billion cubic meters! It's incredible, eh? . . .

—When it comes to numbers, I . . .

—To give you an idea, the construction of the TGV-East railroad quarried 32 million cubic meters of material. Millions! But three-and-a-half billion! The engineers themselves were astonished. Some of them thought the mountain would have to be hollow. It wasn't such a stupid idea, either: an enormous metallic armature and just a thin crust of pebbles and rocks, with glue . . . in places a nice layer of vegetation . . . But that wasn't the idea they went with. Personally I thought this idea wasn't any stupider, but it would have created an underground and a rather nasty kind of space, not easy to restrict, not easy to keep people out of . . . already in the catacombs of the capital lots of mysterious things happen, so, well, I won't go into it. And it would've been very easy to sabotage. So you would've needed a large team of underground cops, and to hide cops is never good, it makes people nervous. All in all, having this big pile of garbage reach 1500 meters finally posed fewer problems, but there was still the problem of quantity . . .

—Bon appetit, Papa.

—Bon appetit, my little girl.

—This smells good.

—Do you have a hearty appetite? That's a sign that you're doing better. That pleases me. You seemed to be enjoying yourself in America. How is your friend doing . . . Stéphane, right?

—Stephen.

—Yes. So?

—Oh, let's talk about something else . . . He has his life . . .

—Ah . . . what do you mean by that?

—I don't completely know. We have to let a little time go by without seeing each other.

—Ah, well . . . you still can't hold on to a man for more than six months?

—That's right.

—What kind of work does he do?

—He sings.

—Oh yeah? And that's going well? You'll have to give me an album . . . But he doesn't sing in French?

—Yes, he does.

—I'll ask at the record store.

—He's not known here.

—You don't have any photos?

—He's a bit wild.

—He's an Indian?

—That's not what I meant!

—Well, it's your business.

—Yes. You still eat just as quickly as ever. Look, I've hardly started . . .

—Habit. With the mess kits, it was like that. When you eat every day out of a mess kit for more than forty years, you can't develop another rhythm. It's impossible.

—Let's ask for another carafe.

—Yes . . .

—It's strange to hear you talk about that, forty years with a mess kit . . . and it was Mama who prepared it?

—Of course, who else?

—You still have your mess kit?

—How do you mean?

—The object.

—They're in the garage. I had seven of them.

—Why seven?

—I don't know. From time to time your mother bought me a new one . . . Like other people buy ties perhaps . . . It's true that it was a nice little detail . . . what color of mess kit was I going to have that day? And then there was the surprise of what there would be to reheat inside of it.

—You always warmed it up?

—Ah, of course, especially in winter, in a double-boiler on a fire at the construction site, on a large piece of metal . . . as long as we had the right to make fires, because after a while, wood and coal, all had to become part of Mountain R. Not allowed to make smoke! Forbidden to burn anything! So we heated the mess kit on the motor of the truck. We put together a little device on the motor to hold the kit. It was Lerebourg who invented it. For two hundred francs, he put it together for each trucker who asked him for it. At the end of two months, there wasn't a truck without one. They had to be airtight, so that the smell of the motor didn't get into the stew.

—There wasn't a company restaurant?

—Yes, of course, for the Bargeco people, served on trays. We would have been able to go, too, but I didn't like it . . . it wasn't cheap. I preferred to have lunch on the run and drink straight from the bottle. It's silly, huh, but on the other hand, I was in the open air. Mountain R . . . it was a bit like our family's winter vacations.

—And the summer ones?

—Our summer vacations . . .

—Don't you miss them?

—Those times? Of course I miss them. I used to have the feeling that I was acting in a film. It was the greatest role of my life.

—So, tell me about a typical day, with all the details!

—What have I been doing for the last hour?

—Yes, but not in any order . . . I need to get the daily routine straight . . .

—Ah, but you're starting to annoy me, darling!

—Papa . . .

—There are limits.

—Stop it! You agreed to answer, and now you're not sticking to it. You haven't changed.

—And you, when you get hold of a bone, you don't let go! You haven't changed either. Unless in spite of everything you've gotten worse?

—What?

—Your situation.

—Papa, don't start . . .

—But it's you who . . .

—STOP!

—Hey!

—What's unusual about what I'm asking you? I won't use your name, you know . . . They have every confidence in me, over there. If I tell them I have reliable sources, they'll take them for reliable sources. I didn't even tell them that my father worked on the construction project. It doesn't concern them.

—I still don't see why they're giving you so much money for that!

—You don't even know how much they pay me. And I can't tell you why they want to know, because I don't know why! I can only imagine! Their sort of business is constantly geared toward doing the *impossible,* that's how they define themselves . . . It's completely crazy; they live ten years in the future in order to know what kind of thing they should invest in. That's all that interests them. So, your mountain . . . the construction project posed a sufficient number of logistical problems . . . You must have made mistakes . . .

—Who do you mean by *you?*

—Yes, well, sure . . . not at your level . . . the Americans want to know if you ran up against big problems or else, if approached in another way . . . how the project was botched, so to speak . . . I don't know . . . perhaps they're considering finishing your mountain themselves in a few years . . . resuming construction . . . like they did for the Panama Canal . . .

—I see . . . In that case, why don't you go see the engineers?

—Because the engineers blew me off, Papa, when I

asked for an interview . . . Now it's impossible to corner even one! It's not surprising. But I'll manage. With what you tell me, I'm beginning to understand the situation better . . . It helps me a lot.

—Oh yes?

—Certainly . . . I'll know how to approach the engineers better next time . . .

—Yeah.

—Go ahead, Papa . . . tell me about your day . . .

—Ha . . . you're depressing the hell out of me with your little routine.

—Come on . . .

— . . .

—Let's have a little cheese.

—Yes . . .

—Go ahead . . .

—Wake up at 4 AM. Have to set the alarm. Your mother hears it before me. She insists on getting up to make me coffee. When I leave, she goes back to sleep. I kiss her . . . I kiss her armpits. It was our custom. If she didn't have her hands behind her head, I put them there. I gave her a kiss on the tuft, while sniffing. I dipped my fingers in. And I left. I sniffed my fingers while the motor warmed up. I took the car out of the garage. Ah, damn.

—What?

—You know . . . she's no longer here . . . No longer here,

that's all … That armpit no longer exists … and there were two of them! And there were things around them! You don't understand? But what do *you* do, with your American?

—The garage, Papa … don't get so worked up.

—Yes … the garage … I pull the car out and I have three-quarters of an hour on the road to get to the other garage, the one with the trucks.

—It isn't far from here, I'd say.

—No, not very … You can see it when the sky is clear.

—The mountain?

—Yes. If it was done, you'd even see it rather well.

—Go on.

—The others arrived. Normally, there was a daily schedule that I'd made in the evening after meeting with the Bargeco people … So, I gave my orders, and they all left for their trucks … me too, in my own … In winter, the boys were gloomy, they didn't say a word. They had tired faces … you would've thought they were leaving for war on the front. But all right, that didn't last long. A true driver gets his energy back as soon as he's in his cab. He remembers what he's doing. That's how I was. A quarter of an hour later, you arrived before the entrance to the construction site. You could make out the black bulk in the early light … when there wasn't fog … If you'd left empty that morning, the deal was that you went in the direction of the filler; for instance, there might be a consignment of various sorts of trash. Then you put the trucks in single file . . . a crane loaded them . . . You drove past a desk where they noted your number and the cubic feet . . . And then off to the peak! That was the best moment . . . I would put on a little music, or the news, and during a certain time of the year you were treated to a little bit of sunrise. It wasn't bad. Anyway, I never got tired of it. The ascent was a lot more irritating because the road's shoulders, which normally were stable . . . they moved more than a little, especially when it rained, or at the end of winter, during the thaw. In the morning, the first trip, it was still okay, because there weren't trucks coming down, but later in the day, you had to pass them on the way up . . . in dry weather, you were guaranteed to get dust in your nose. There were risks. Having arrived at the top, you dumped it all. In general you followed the plan, the lots were numbered . . . There was radio contact. When I say "at the top," obviously it was an immense plateau, since the base began at 700 hectares . . . so, considering the slope, two years passed before you could truly speak of a little summit, but because they'd dug all around it to use the dirt that was close by, that then became ground zero, so-called sea level . . . anyway that created the effect of height rather quickly, especially from one side . . . The first two hundred meters didn't take long . . . and that was what was always photographed, the south face. So, up on the mountain, on the day I'm talking about, you'd still be at 400 or 500 meters . . . It's not nothing . . . But it's true that in the center of the plateau, up top, there was a big hole, because it wasn't all filled, far from it. First they very carefully made the edges, a bit like a dyke, you know, and then in the middle there was something like a crater, and you filled it as best you could, when you could, with garbage or rubble . . . It depended on who'd sold their damn . . . Anyway, that's how tons of public garbage dumps were emptied to fill that fucking mountain . . . it wasn't necessarily a bad idea . . . lots of industrial waste dumps as well . . . I remember seeing barrels arrive by helicopter . . . at the end of a cable under the helicopter . . . I wish I knew for sure that it wasn't nuclear waste . . . Well. Anyway, I was mainly hauling things . . . For example when they smashed apart the city of Trente à La Chapelle, I was the one who salvaged everything, with my guys, after the explosions. I was with Jeannot who . . . come to think of it . . . he came from there. He spent all his childhood there. He was like a madman! Concrete, scrap metal, scrap metal, concrete . . . not easy, but okay, I was up to it . . . It was later that I did the slag heaps. So, on the day I was talking about, I was up on the mountain and there's a cargo of tires . . . a large quantity . . . I'd never seen so many tires in my life. So, the problem was to spread them around. There couldn't be a whole section of the mountain made of tires. Not stable enough. You can figure that out without being there. So, a truckload here, a truckload there, and mix in some loose stones. They even used the barriers that they use to make dams now, that kind of concrete star-like thing . . . What do you call them? Tetrapods . . . it was good material but it cost too much . . . and was very heavy . . . They were reserved for spots that were a little delicate. So, when you arrived up above, in the glow of the headlights, in the dust the trucks made, a night of rain and fog—or else, with the mid-afternoon storms, under a sky that was black, black, black . . . If hell exists, it must look like that . . . as like that as two drops of water . . . and incidentally there wasn't any drinkable water up there . . . so you were thirsty, and you drank all your beer . . . The same thing in summer, because it's a furnace. Each day you made at least five round trips. If you did more, you got a bonus, but careful, not at the risk of safety! There were informers among the truckers, and you better believe the trucks were inspected.

—But then how was Di Pascale, for instance, able to be overloaded?

—That was much later . . . After a while, you found a system, schemes were created . . . he must have bribed the supervisor. You can always buy someone, somewhere! You pay the price and don't think about the consequences.

—To pay off someone in order to work more!

—Ah, yes . . .

59

—But what was the advantage to being overloaded?

—To save one trip out of every ten, if you have filler to finish all by yourself ... or else, with the help of the guy who keeps the records, you count a trip you don't make ... It was complicated, you were paid by the trip and by the cubic meter, there were two graphs ... Let's not go into it ...

—Did it pay well?

—Di Pascale perhaps bought a little bit too luxurious a house, and so then, inevitably, he wanted to earn more. But that was later on. As for me, I was doing nothing more than temporary jobs by that time. The mountain started to take shape a little bit. We celebrated 650 meters ... cheating a little ... cheating a lot ... The celebration had been planned for the 750 meter mark, the project half finished ... it was just before the elections ... but even cheating we couldn't celebrate higher than 650 ... It wasn't 650 everywhere ... and it was said that they wouldn't even have 600 meters before long ...

—Why?

—Settling ... When the land was chosen, there were a lot of parameters: the ground couldn't be too compressible—too soft—and then, on the other hand, it couldn't pose too many problems for transferring materials. As a result, the ground didn't have an equal density everywhere, in spots there was clay, there was mud, peat ... So, there was a forseeable sinkage, in other words it sunk a little . . . Well, because it all weighed a hell of a lot! It should have been lightened, Mountain R, loaded with cork or styrofoam balls . . . I dreamed about that at night . . . about lightening it. It became an obsession.

—I understand . . .

—There was already a . . . what do you call it? A cable car with a hopper for the materials, but that didn't work for long . . . bicable aerial transport . . . the good old truck remains irreplaceable . . . the cable-line was used for visitors, but that didn't work for long either . . . scared the hell out of them . . . a reception for officials, up above, and the press . . . And besides, the visits soon became rare, because having tourists was more annoying than anything else. They pretended to be impressed, but behind our backs they were cynical . . . And then came—here we are—Di Pascale's accident. Fortunately, it was night.

—Why fortunately?

—Yes, no . . . I said *fortunately?* . . . It was Bargeco's boys who said *fortunately* . . . It was easier for giving aid . . .

—I don't see how.

—It's what they said.

—Yes?

—Yes.

—Let's maybe go have some coffee at the house. What do you think?

—Oh, yes, let's go back. I have an old bottle of Calvados. So, you really want to pay the bill?

—Yes, yes.

—The sky's overcast. It's colder. Well, thanks! It's been a long time since I haven't had to pay for a meal! No, go that way . . .

—You're right, it isn't far.

—A stone's throw.

—You go there every day?

—Oh, they're very nice.

—They seem like it. Your dog doesn't get bored?

—Oh no, but he's happy to see me again. He knows quite well what's in store for him after lunch . . . Look . . . there's still one in my pocket . . . But of course I came back . . . He's happy . . . That's enough. Time to lie down. I'll let you make the coffee, if you don't mind.

—Of course.

—The coffee . . . and the post-coffee liquor.

—Here, Papa.

—No, no sugar! It doesn't agree with me . . . You never have news of your cousin Noël? I'll have Calva.

—Noël? No, never. That's all in the past.

—I'd very much like to see him again. He was a courageous little boy . . . He had an accident, didn't he?

—I think so, yes.

—He raced motorcycles . . .

—Probably.

—This Calva is really good. You don't want any?

—No.

—Your mother really liked . . .

—The Calva?

—No . . . the cousin. Noël . . . She would have liked to hire him, but personally I didn't want to work with family on the construction site.

—Mama wasn't family?

—Yes, but she stayed at the office, at the house . . . Family and job sites shouldn't mix.

—I understand. Where were we? You were talking about giving aid for Di Pascale's accident . . . You were speaking as if there had been fifty dead . . .

—Me?

—Yes.

— . . .

—I'm listening!

—There were at least three or four hundred.

—What?

—Yes. If not more . . .

—Oh . . .

—Yes.

—Umm . . . you don't mean there were three or four hundred people *in his truck?*

—No, not that . . . but he fell onto the camp.

—Oh shit!

—Yeah, it was a Friday evening . . . It was pouring rain. But even though it was bad weather . . . I have never told this to anyone. Di Pascale was driving with his truck full of glass. I was behind him in my truck, carrying glass too. Except there was no fucking reason for me to be there. I was retired, and I was a widower. A brand-new widower. So, to keep from drinking all day long, I went to give Di Pascale a hand . . . not even for the money, just to keep busy . . .

—You were overloaded too?

—Oh yes, just as much!

—Go on!

—And it's then that things gave way under Di Pascale's wheels . . . the rain, the weakened roads, the overloading . . . I saw the mountain part, a fault opening up in that pile of custard, and I saw the fault move toward me like a big stroke of a carpenter's pencil, quite straight . . . you have the impression of a blade of nothingness that's searching for you, that's chosen you in particular to skin alive . . . Then, by reflex, just when I saw Di Pascale's truck tipping, I opened my door and I jumped. Jeannot was next to me, and he was thrown through the windshield just at the moment when the truck slipped down. I hurtled down twenty meters without hitting much, dirt in my eyes and up my nostrils . . . finally, the ground . . . shitty ground, yes! there were even chips of glass . . . it smelled like shit . . . and then I found Jeannot . . .

—Jeannot? I thought you'd lost track of him . . . That's what you said before . . . Then it wasn't true . . .

—Did I say that?

—Yes. He was with you? He was . . . dead?

—Oh, no. He was stunned. Quite stunned, but not a scratch . . . well, yes, scratches, obviously, on account of going through the windshield. But he knew exactly what was below us. It was the Turkish encampment. See, Jeannot was a queer. I've never understood that sort, but okay . . . that wasn't what I wanted him for, myself . . . We made fun of him just a little from time to time. So, when he understood that the camp was just below, he wanted to go down the mountainside, which was madness, obviously, and strictly forbidden then, because of the risk of landslide . . . and there was barbed wire every hundred meters! It rained, rained, rained, all that the sky could rain, it was terrifying how much rain the sky had that night! Within two minutes we were soaked to the bone; we'd lost our trucks and Di Pascale . . . and Jeannot had come unhinged . . . He was afraid of what had happened below . . . and he had good reason to be . . . because landslide and run-off had completely saturated the drainage canals, and there was an avalanche, an avalanche of our shit, worse than an avalanche of snow . . . on a night when the Turks weren't working . . . they were Muslims, in fact, carefully gathered for some kind of strange event . . . it might even have been Ramadan . . . their version of Lent . . . you get the picture. You couldn't descend any further, but he tried . . . He shouted a name, I remember: "Nazim! Nazim! . . ." I tried to reason with him . . . It's true . . . Why didn't he shout "Di Pascale! Di Pascale!" and why didn't I call out to Di Pascale? But all his shouting was useless, as useless as opening an umbrella to shelter all of Mountain R! I had to almost knock him out and take him up again on my back, and for every two meters I gained on the slope, I lost three, and I really believed we were going to get stuck there, both of us. Shit. I was panting like an old seal. Fortunately, I had good shoes with stiff soles . . . Finally, after having wandered for more than an hour, I think we must have simply drifted along the mountainside; in other words we hadn't gained an inch of altitude—just the opposite—but we hadn't lost too much either, and we ended up finding the packed trail again, which was completely torn up by the flow of all kinds of trash and by buckets of rain. I was sure that I would never see Di Pascale again . . . I don't know why, because I didn't have any proof . . . I was sure he was dead. And he *was* dead. I never saw him again.

—Hmmm . . .

—My problem was that I had no business being there. In fact, if I was nabbed they could have thought that I was stealing someone else's work, which was frowned upon . . . it could wreck my retirement. You already didn't know from one month to the next if you were going to receive your check. To go back down on foot the five or six kilometers that separated me from the parking lot below wasn't easy, especially with a crazed Jeannot in tow. I held him by the wrist, so I wouldn't lose him. If I'd walked past the checkpoint, I would have been spotted immediately . . .

—But, driving up, they'd let you go by . . .

—Yes, but they didn't know it was me. It was Di Pascale's crew, Di Pascale's truck . . . They looked the other way . . . But then, after what had happened . . . In short, it was a complete fuck-up, the worst situation imaginable: an accident at work when you're not following the rules!

—So, what happened?

—From up there, you couldn't climb down the side any further. Had anyone down below realized what had happened? Not sure . . . There was nothing else to do but go down the trail on foot. Jeannot still brayed like a mule for his Nazim! We walked like that . . . I don't know . . . maybe a kilometer and a half . . . And that was when we saw one of the Land Rovers of the Bargeco boys coming. You couldn't help recognizing them, even from far away, especially when you'd done everything to avoid them for years.

—So?

—So, I said to Jeannot that we needed to hide. That we had to let them pass. Bite our lips and, once they'd gone, continue down the mountain. They must have been out for blood, though, because accident or no, weather like that was a month of work blown, what with the run-off . . . I thought that Jeannot understood all that . . . At first, he agreed to hide . . . out of habit . . . And anyway I was holding him. But when the headlights approached, he got loose and threw himself in front of them. The cars stopped, and the squad climbed down. He started to tell them about the fall of the two trucks, the probable ava-lanche, and what was most likely underneath. I was wor-ried he was going to tell them about me. Fortunately, it was hard to understand Jeannot, with his speech problem . . . The others already knew what was going on, obviously . . . There was one who yelled out: "But how does this guy know about that?"—"Nazim!"—"Shut up," said another, "don't talk about that. You're already in trouble, you have no busi-ness here . . . " But Jeannot insisted: "It's the Turk camp, hey, it's the Turk camp that took it smack in the face! My friends are down there, you're going to get them back for me, my friends!" But Jeannot was making his appeal to one of the worst leaders of the gang. He took him by the shoulders and clung to him like a cat to a tree trunk. And the wind-shield wipers of the three Rovers squealed, trying desper-ately to sweep away the pounding rain. So, the gang leader pushed Jeannot to the ground and kicked him between the eyes. There was a crunch. He already had a deformed face, poor kid! The guy had kicked so hard that he must have hurt his foot, because he started limping. He climbed back up into the cab and came out again with a weapon, a rifle, I didn't know anything about guns . . . a rifle with a scope . . . and he yelled out that, yes, the Turk camp was covered over and that there were a lot of dead under the shit and mud, but that since no one was supposed to talk about it and since Jeannot didn't look very capable of keeping quiet . . . Then he fired two shots into Jeannot, who was already on the ground and so didn't have far to fall. A rifle with a scope . . . he wasn't five meters away . . . he didn't have to use the scope to aim . . . if he had, he would've seen him larger than life . . . They threw him into the Land Rover and left. I continued to walk, looking behind me from time to time in case they came back. They couldn't do anything *other* than come back, because soon they were going to stumble onto the landslide . . . So, when they came, I hid again. I'm sure they must have taken the time to toss Jeannot into the hole . . . and when I got down to the bottom, I took to the drainage canals . . . In all the commotion, nobody saw me. There was a string of firemen, riot police, watchmen, who didn't really know what to do . . . Miraculously, I hadn't parked my car in the lot that night because I didn't trust the guy at the entrance. So, I left without being seen or recognized.

—Okay, go on . . .

—I took my car . . . I think I rolled along at ten kilometers an hour. It must have been two o'clock in the morning . . . I was trembling. I was soaked through and covered with mud. You know where I went? Right away, without thinking?

—No.

—I went to the cemetery. I went to say hello . . .

—Papa . . .

—I went to say goodnight to your mother.

—Really?

—It's foolish to cry outdoors, where all the world can see. But when the sky pours down rain on you, you hardly notice.

— . . .

—I went to give her a kiss . . . She consoled me. I knew that she'd agree to wake up, considering the seriousness of the situation . . . I hadn't even brought flowers . . . It didn't matter. How thin her voice had become! . . . but I recognized her from her way of stretching . . . She told me: you shouldn't do it, my darling . . . Stop, now. Relax a little. Get busy with the garden, take care of my dahlias and my hydrangeas . . . Think more and more about me . . . Think a little more about yourself . . . Let them finish their dungheap on their own . . . I'm watching you, you know, from above . . . I tuck you into our bed . . . I remind you that you need to take your medicine . . . I look at you every day as you get dressed: I never miss that. I open my arms . . . Don't you feel it when I open my arms? Aren't I there on top of you when you jerk-off? Why are you still driving that damned truck? Just stay near the fireplace and look at our wedding pictures . . . Go on, don't cry anymore, and let's not catch cold now and get bronchitis . . . How well she spoke!

—She always found just the right words . . .

—Have you been there at least? To the cemetery?

—It's not All Saints' Day!

—You should go there anyway . . . We'll both go . . . What a night, good God . . . what a night that was! I stayed there until daybreak . . . and I didn't even manage to catch my death of a cold.

—Fortunately!

—Why I went there, you understand . . . you could wonder . . . it was for her, obviously . . . She'd always given good advice . . . But it was also because I knew that I could never go to Di Pascale's burial. And I liked Di Pascale a lot.

—Why couldn't you go to Di Pascale's funeral?

—Because he hadn't had an accident! Don't you get it? Are you even listening? He'd never existed, Di Pascale . . . They bought Mrs. Di Pascale's silence, but she wouldn't even have the right to be a widow. Superior interest of the State! There never was any catastrophe on the construction site of Mountain R! Isn't it clear?

—Oh yes, it's clear!

—Everyone knew that the access roads were a little haphazard . . . At least not developed compared to how high they wanted the mountain to be . . . It had to happen . . .

—It happened . . .

—Bargeco started to lose money on Mountain R . . . in any case, that's what they said. So, since for this job they were associated with Bouton Ltd., Bouton became more and more involved in the control of Mountain R. And during that time Bargeco sent its best minds to Colombia and Saudi Arabia where gigantic construction projects were starting as well . . . Bouton Ltd. wasn't as serious as Bargeco . . . What was I saying before?

—You were at the cemetery . . .

—Ah, yes . . . I came back here. I had a craving for croissants . . . You can't imagine . . . but in the state I was in . . . I wasn't going to show myself at the bakery . . . Then, I don't know what came over me, I phoned the baker . . . I knew him well, I'd been his customer for thirty years . . . I asked him to deliver thirty of the day's croissants, and to leave them under the porch roof, in front of the door. He didn't need to be afraid, the dog would be tied up. It must have seemed like a pregnant woman's request . . . He didn't pry. I had my thirty warm croissants . . . the dog howled like a madman . . . It was seven o'clock in the mourner . . . hmm, in the roaming, ah! morning! and I put myself under the showerhead like a cup that you want to wash without getting your hands wet . . . I slipped into my bathrobe, and after I made myself a cup of coffee, no, I made myself *two liters* of coffee, yes, it was two liters . . . I poured it into a soup tureen . . . damn, I was thirsty . . . and I started to dip my croissants in the shou . . . soup tureen, and I felt the steam of the coffee dampening my forehead and my two-day growth of beard. Why are you looking at me like that? What would you have done in my place, huh?

—I don't know what I would have done, Papa.

—Of course . . .

—What were you thinking about?

—I thought that it was better for me that Jeannot was dead . . . because Jeannot wouldn't have been able to keep quiet, and I would have been in trouble. And anyway, that boy was unlucky. He never had a chance, he had to die there, at Mountain R. And it was better that Di Pascale was dead, because they would have tortured him to find out who drove the second truck.

—You thought that . . . with your mouth full . . .

—Yes. You don't know what it's like to eat thirty croissants, when you crave croissants, and when the croissants and the coffee make you want to retch, because croissants, they're like your wife's flesh, and your wife's flesh is all gone . . . And those damn croissants, I knew that I had to eat every last one. They were snakes, whole snakes, which the mountain had cooked up just for me. Mountain R was

there to give birth to those snakes, which were only for me
. . . you understand that? Born only so that I could swallow them from head to tail . . . your father . . . I didn't succeed in finishing them off, my sna . . . my croissants. And
then, the next minute I puked it all into the soup tureen
. . .

—Oh . . .

—Yeah . . .

—Aunt Georgette's soup tureen?

—Yes, that's the one.

—And . . . the others?

—What others?

—All the people who were under the landslide . . . you
told me hundreds.

—Oh yeah.

—That's all you care about it?

—I'm going to tell you something, my dear, something your grandfather used to say: it's better to kick than
be kicked.

—Is that so?

—See for yourself . . .

—Don't touch me! Don't touch me! . . .

—Oh! Well . . .

—And leave that Calva alone, now! That's enough!

—Let go of that bottle!

—No.

—Watch yourself . . .

—You're drunk!

—Leave me alone.

—Oh, God! . . . Here's what we're going to do, Papa . . . you're going to be rewarded with . . . what do they call it? A "backward glass of spirits"?

—What's that?

—You don't remember? It was one of Mama's expressions, no? Put your head in cold water. Otherwise, you're really going to start acting like you used to, and I don't want that.

—That's what you think?

—I'm sure of it.

—Don't talk about your mother . . .

—If I want to . . .

—Your boyfriend, he doesn't drink? You stop him from drinking? It's no surprise that there's such a distance between you . . .

—Come on, Papa, we'll drink more after . . .

—After what?

—The sink's this way.

—Okay.

—Bend over!

—Brrrrr!

—There . . .

—Damn . . .

—So? How was it?

—Cold.

—Feeling better?

—Yeah.

—Come on, let's sit back down. You're going to have some more strong coffee.

—Yes. Thanks . . . that's how I know I'm getting old. It's good that you're here.

—Dry yourself off.

—There . . .

—Now . . . how did you get the deal?

—What?

—How did you get the deal?

—Back to this again?

—You're going to answer me, yes? How did you get the deal?

—Won't you just leave me alone?

—Out of the question.

—The interview's over.

—It's just started.

—No, well who is this insipid bitch who shows up to piss off her father? . . . Will you please get out of my house . . .

—*Your* house . . . but it's as much my house as yours . . . right, poor displaced old man! Just because you spilled a few tears on your fake-marble coffee table and your carpet, you . . .

—You're asking for it! You're asking for it! Get out!

—Not before you tell me how you got it, that rotten deal for that rotten project of a rotten mountain that poisoned my childhood and the entire Republic!

—But how could I have gotten this deal, you wonder? You think I was able to get it honestly? Of course not! There is no honest deal with things like this, little girl! No, and by what miracle did your Yanks manage to hire *you*? It isn't possible! Do you think that your little buddies are any different? What am I supposed to believe? That with you they hired little miss perfect? That you didn't have to sleep with someone for that nice salary of yours?

—Forget about your lectures! I want to know how, how, how! Why do you think I'm going to judge you? I just want to know, that's all! Do you think I give a damn about the sainted image of my father?

—Bitch!

—Thanks! It seems we're making real progress! So? What were these bribes? Whose ass did you kiss?

—You idiot! I wasn't rich enough to afford bribes. But I had something else. I had better than that.

—What?

—Connections.

—What kind?

—Shady.

—With whom?

—With the highest there is.

—The president?

—Of the Council! of the Republic!

—That scum!

—What do you know of that gentleman to turn him so easily into scum?

—More than you think.

—I did him some favors, believe it or not. At a time before you were even born. Well, not him personally . . . never met him . . . but his recruiters, yes.

—You were in his party?

—No. I was more useful outside. He preferred that I be outside . . . Unofficially, it was called the Captaincy. There's nothing worse than being forced to renounce what you know how to do, I mean what you know how to do easily, work well done . . . for something that pays a lot but that doesn't feel good . . . but what can you do? Repaying debts can become an obsession, taxes, social security . . . all the business expenses . . . all the crap you can't escape from. So either your wife leaves you for someone who's better off and you turn into a bum, or else you do things . . .

—What sorts of things?

—Things that are a little tricky, sensitive . . .

—Not the . . .

—No! How can you think that? Is there anything you

won't say? No . . . Just scare certain people who might say things . . . destroy certain secrets. That's all. Ask some people to forget things they know, help them get rid of papers, use those papers to light a fire under the logs in the fireplace of their summer house. I did that many times, discreetly . . . not in front of them . . . But it wasn't for me . . . I was scared stiff when I had to force my way into those places, breaking and entering with a flashlight . . . They ended up understanding that it wasn't from ill will that . . . that they could get me to do what they wanted, provided I drove my truck. So, I trafficked, in things across several borders. I did pretty well.

—What were you carrying?

—Things . . .

—Cash? Drugs? Explosives?

—No, no, *things* . . . I didn't even know what they were. I should have known. I would have kept quiet much better . . . And then, very quickly, there was no longer any need for me. The closer they got to power, the more they professionalized their crews. So I returned to my trade. It would have been a bit sad without this tale of the mountain to spice things up. I'm certain I was wrong in telling you all this. It'll come back to haunt me one day.

—No, you don't have to be afraid of me. Go on . . . I want to know more.

—Careful!

—Would you stop drinking!

—Are you sure you're ready to hear all I could tell you? Everything I've been keeping in my head?

—That's why I'm here.

—Things that concern you directly?

—What do I have to do with the construction site?

—Oh! You're starting to get defensive . . .

—What are you planning to make up?

—Make up, nothing, but simply tell you the true story that almost caused your mother and me to separate, something that I couldn't bear and that led to your going to Switzerland.

—My Swiss exile.

—You've always liked colorful phrases. Like your mother. But your mother had learned to distrust herself. I'm the one who taught her that. You want to hear or not?

—No, shut up!

—It was springtime. Do you remember? There was still construction going on here, in the house. Your mother was sick. A bad case of the flu. A high fever. She kept sweating all over our bed. I stopped changing the sheets. One night, it disgusted me. I don't know why it happened that night . . . I couldn't stand it anymore. I was exhausted. But I couldn't sleep. I had a hard-on. I felt dirty. She was delirious. The evening before, we'd made love even with her fever, and in a certain way it had been terrific, like fucking a cow or a female bear . . . or a mountain . . . She was much clumsier than usual, a big warm-blooded beast, sticky and hot, sprawled on top of me . . .

—Warm-blooded beast? You've no right to speak of her like that!

—Shut up! She'd found the energy to climb on top of me . . . She didn't know what she was doing.

—You're drunk. Shut up.

—The next night, I was completely obsessed by this horny memory of the night before. But your mother had taken sleeping pills and she was deep asleep, snoring . . . I really tried to wake her up, but she clenched herself forcefully, ass, thighs, arms, closed herself off, still snoring like a house on fire, and that made me mad, and the fever, the heat, the sweat . . . all of that suddenly nauseated me, so I went out into the garden, completely naked . . . It was quiet, we didn't have a dog yet . . . and I took a shower under the cherry tree, that one over there, which wasn't as big as it is today. A cold shower, with the garden hose, but it didn't make my hard-on go down an inch. That's when I went to your window. You had your night-light on, your stupid baby-who's-afraid-of-the-dark night-light . . .

—Shut up.

—You've always encouraged the idea that you slept so soundly that your father's truck could pass over your body

81

without waking you . . . that was what we said at the house for years, and whenever you heard that phrase you smiled, as if you were waiting for that moment. And I was overflowing with desire to fuck the whole world that night . . . forced by I don't know what thirst. I shoved open your unlocked window. I simply lifted my legs through your window, which wasn't all that high up, and in passing my thighs over the sill I saw my cock move from the garden into your room, my cock which seemed to me to be holding up well, still erect, still throbbing. The light from the street illuminated your little sleeping body and your head, which seemed to be whispering to that threadbare bunny you clung to. Your legs had pushed back the sheets, and you offered me all your innocence, which I spread open a little, gasping for breath. I had a crazy desire to enter you, a little virgin, yet I knew I wouldn't do anything like that. But I had to do something. I heard drops of water, the water from my shower, falling onto the linoleum floor. Then I thought about how cats, lions, and cows lick their young all over their bodies and in all their folds, and that here was a practice to be embraced by higher minds. I started to lick you between your legs, where pubic hair was growing which, to my tongue, seemed impossibly fine. Slowly, I tried to go further, without hurting you, with the benefit of this paternal oiling, this lube job, and there was no reason to see this as wrong. You didn't even wake up, but you groaned with pleasure. The prediction had been proven correct: your father's truck would have no influence over your sleep. I shot my load under your bed, with more pleasure than I had ever had. And that was when I heard a noise. Your mother came in the room, face flushed, still just as feverish. She was looking for me, and seemed to understand what was going on. But you were no longer sleeping, were you?

—...

—Now's not the time to cry, my darling. I *know* that you were no longer sleeping, hadn't been for a while, but I didn't betray you to your mother. I never told her that you might have enjoyed it. Which didn't prevent me from being found naked in my daughter's room, admittedly with less of a hard-on, which still may have had a drop on the tip, and of course your mother saw all these things. When I tried to accompany her back to bed, telling her tenderly (and I didn't restrain my feelings) that she mustn't catch cold, I felt that she was as unhappy as if she'd found me with another woman. And even though I'd kind of fucked you, that didn't stop me, fifteen minutes later, from refucking her as she wept her fevered tears. The next day, your departure was arranged. You would finish your studies in the mountains, in Switzerland.

—Mountain S.

—It's true, we called it that . . .

—She was the one who decided?

83

—I was the one who proposed it. The money was there.

—I didn't know I was educated with such dirty money.

—No dirtier than any other.

—Entrusted with laundering it . . .

—Fancy phrases are always wrong, you know.

—Daughter of a truck . . . I'm the daughter of an adipose, hairy sweating truck. I want to sell my father to the highest bidder. Or to send him to a garbage dump.

—Let him instead be bored to death with his dog in his suburban home.

—What were you involved in?

—I was involved in work. And I have seen a lot more of it than I've told you. I was happy. Happy, when I drove in brand-new workers, very cheerful workers, who sang . . . who even danced in the back . . . There was a poster of the period with my truck in the photo, I still have it somewhere . . . a motivational poster . . . a closeup of a smile and some big muscles . . . Happy, for example, when we salvaged an entire district of Châtillon which was still inhabited by 200 squatters . . . There, we didn't even have the cops to help us. We went directly there with our own trucks. Blowing our horns, we went straight to the first wall of whatever house was in front of us and tore it open. I'd installed a sort of metallic battering ram at the front of my truck. That must have been terrifying. It made the families flee . . .

—This bastard won't shut up!

—We handled it so as not to hurt anyone, OK? We targeted a house on the outskirts, one which was more or less empty. And we never made the least mistake. There were even some kids who approached us after that, looking for work. They came to us on their own! That's what Mountain R was all about. Sometimes we even got attached to our garbage . . . in the good times, we sorted through it, we put the best stuff aside, we knew how to appreciate it like a horse dealer appreciates a good horse . . . we stroked it with our hands, we caressed it . . . we took it away with a little bit of force, true . . . some objects really pleased us . . . and we kept those for special purposes. We had fun and we made some money! When we did demolition, it was terrible . . . We had the impression that we were going to make a real piece of the mountain, simple and spectacular . . . But once you'd dumped it at the construction site, you could hardly see it. So we set out again to be loaded up, each time a bit more determined.

—Did mother know all that?

—No, she knew nothing about *all that*. She never knew anything about *all that*.

—How is that possible? I don't believe you.

—Like an ostrich. Head in the sand.

—In the sand of your truck's bucket . . .

—There wasn't usually sand in my bucket. Sand was

too expensive . . . too expensive for Mountain R.

—Poor dead woman . . .

—She died thanking me.

—For what?

—For having worked without getting tired . . . without getting tired of life and without getting tired of her. And capable of raising a child, of paying for her studies, so that she might speak English and ride horses. Thankful that we never lacked meat, milk and vegetables. Isn't that a great success? You found work with the English that I paid for. You don't seem to appreciate this. You don't seem grateful.

—I'm finding things out.

—That was the deal. We'd become trash pickers. It was our only obsession. Knights of Filler, Captain Rubbish, General Shit . . . especially since we were interested in what we found, understand? . . . because eventually Bargeco wasn't necessarily in the best situation to bargain. We had to be careful, because when Bargeco showed up under his own name, people sold us their piles of trash as if they were gold. And if he haggled them down, people got annoyed and covered the trash with their bodies . . . Nobodies like us, when we found a trail, we didn't talk about Mountain R, we got there slowly: nothing had value. We paid from out of the back of the truck and we were reimbursed at the back of the truck . . . dependable from start to finish . . . but we took a little something in the process. Incidentally, we didn't do a bad job of cleaning up the Republic. There was only one time when I refused a load. Opaque canisters. I'm sure they were full of something dangerous . . . bioxin? Does that exist, bioxin?

—Dioxin . . . yes, that exists. And it is dangerous.

—Ah, well, there were hundreds of barrels to scavenge in an abandoned factory, near La Ferté something or other.

—So, you refused?

—Well, I got sick . . .

—Ah! that explains it . . .

—All the same, I didn't go. It was Lerebourg who did it. In the end they didn't have any unusual problems. You look tired, darling.

—He got sick! Not even the balls to say no! That's my father . . . Yes, I'm exhausted . . . It's as if you'd beaten me for five hours . . .

—And you stay . . . You're not leaving . . . What are you waiting for me to tell you? I have nothing more. I won't feed you any more. I won't furnish you with any more little secrets. I've run dry. Incidentally, I'm not going to put off dying, you'll be happy to know. You won't have to lie down near my body and tell me to wake up . . . That's what I did with your mother, I tried to shake her out of it for two days, and I still have her carrion stench in my nostrils! But I didn't succeed in making her come back, and then they put her in a wooden box in the ground. I wanted to crush their skulls. There was even someone who held me round the waist while they clamped down the goddam lid and sealed it. Again something you didn't know, since you weren't there. Not even at your own mother's burial!

—You know very well that I was too far away, and that I couldn't call.

—Yeah, yeah . . .

—Oh, and then you go and harass me about it. Do you think that not being there stopped me from crying as soon as I knew?

—Me, I knew right away. I wasn't at home when she died. I wasn't beside her, but I knew right away. I felt it in my gut. It was obvious. I looked at the time, and it made sense . . . a sinking feeling in my stomach . . . I was driving.

—Oh, come on!

—You have never been sensitive . . .

—No, no, of course not! . . .

—Never saw any of what was happening outside of your little life of a lazy, spoiled, insipid bitch . . .

—Is that what you think? Well, I too have something that I know and haven't told *you*.

—I'm not asking you for anything.

—One day, before the earrings . . . You'll understand why I was extremely sad during the earring dinner . . . I came back from school early, because a teacher was sick . . .

And, I don't know why, I too stopped at the window before coming in . . . While you were off on your mountain, obviously, climbing your mountain, during that time another mountaineer was climbing on your wife!

—You little bitch!

—Because of what you told me a few minutes ago about your disgusting attack on me, you'll listen to me as well, you *will* listen to me! Di Pascale . . . of course, Di Pascale . . . I lied to you before . . . I haven't forgotten who Di Pascale was . . . Di Pascale was on top of your wife, on top of my mother, planted in her like a flag . . . with tufts of hair on his shoulders and all over his lower back . . .

—It's not true . . . Di Pascale . . .

— . . . and she, she kept her eyes closed, as if oblivious to his pleasure but enveloped in her own, on the ground, on the carpet, her fat flesh emerging from her disheveled clothes . . . Two animals there, two bugs, who had nothing to say to each other, except from the noise of their bodies. I saw it myself before leaving for Switzerland. I saw her as I see you. You're staying rather calm!

—You little bitch!

—If you hit me . . . dirty cuckold, cuckold, cuckold! I'll scream!

—Calm down a little. Me, I fucked Di Pascale's wife, if you want to know.

—This is getting sick . . . Wasn't there anyone else to

fuck? Did all your lives revolve around the Mountain or what?

—And you, I wonder, what do you revolve around?

—Answer me!

—Yeah, that's exactly it . . . it was all we lived for . . . We were drugged by the same diesel fuel, the same exhaust fumes . . . the same brutal tasks, the same cadences, the same bookkeeping columns! Crazy, we were crazy! Attached to Mountain R! Can you understand that?

—All too well!

—Damn!

— . . .

— . . .

—You didn't think you could pull it off?

—Pull what off?

—Mountain R . . . Don't tell me you were already dreaming of the brochure with the ski trails traced in colors on a map, with hotels and one-room flats for sale!

—Yes! Exactly . . . I'd even . . . you're going to find me very naive . . . I'd even deposited money for the purchase of an apartment at 1100 meters. Facing south, balcony, fireplace, view of the river. Your mother dreamed of it! I gave 1500 francs every month. We were one of the many . . . today in legal action, the company is bankrupt. I'll get nothing back at all. These delays . . . oh! these delays . . . they made me so goddamn mad! You know, twenty years earlier I would have done it alone, their mountain, without publicity, without propaganda, in silence and hard work. I was capable of doing it, without any desire for money, and avoiding losing all this time with thugs who didn't really care if they finished it or not, who thought only of stuffing their pockets full, abusing their workers and sneaking in hustlers . . . they understood the distractions, the attractions . . . those selfish, cold, calculating bastards! But me, I dreamed about it every night. I liked its design, all the contours the architect had designed. I still have a poster somewhere around here . . . I liked the little red light at its summit to greet the airplanes. I didn't have the right connections, that's all! I wasn't important enough, and when I wrote to the president to explain all that to him, it was already too late, he was starting to crumble under the scandals. He'd been tricked straight down the line by the people around him . . . It's always like that.

—Even so, you're not going to defend him . . .

—In his place, I would have gotten rid of all those useless people. I would have used their dry bones to gain another meter of filler for Mountain R . . . And stable filler, good grit of bone, on which you could run all the special slaloms of the Winter Games!

—Well, you'd certainly have avoided some problems! But I have the feeling that this mountain is already quite a lovely mass grave . . .

—It's always the same thing . . . it was much better with the opposition . . . With the opposition, there was truly a leader. I heard him speak, off the cuff, to crowds that didn't love him . . . and he turned them around in no time at all, simply in thinking only of what he had to tell them, in putting all his force into it, in speaking of everything and nothing . . . but he never lost sight of his objective. He had a beautiful deep voice. He always spoke standing up. When you're the leader, you get weak. It can't be helped. You're obliged to pass the tiller on to others. And then the others betray you, even without knowing it, by gossiping, and you lap up their words, and after you've lapped them up, you piss them somewhere into a hole that doesn't know how to hold its damn tongue . . .

—Why is your dog barking?

—How should I know?

—He's answering when you yell.

—It's not that . . .

—Visitors?

—Yeah. The police?

—You'd think so . . . It doesn't seem to concern you very much.

—It's nothing, I was waiting for them. Wait . . . let me give you . . . They still have really shitty cars, the police . . . It's a simple summons. I'm not going to panic over that. I know the police well. They'd already warned me . . . I thought it would be next week . . . You'll have to make them a little coffee. I'm coming! Come in, come in . . . he won't bite you! He's happy to howl, but look at his tail . . . Wouldn't hurt a burglar . . . ha ha ha! I'll open the door for you . . . One minute . . . I have my daughter . . . A sort of judge wants me to tell what I know . . . I won't tell them as much as I told you. Although . . . here, take this envelope. It's for you. I'm telling you to take it! Put it in your pocket. I don't know much. I have nothing to be ashamed of. Besides, they summoned me in the proper fashion, and respectfully. You don't have to blush for your old father. I'm not a nobody. I'm an old fighter from Mountain R.

III

The Trial
(short excerpt)

It is the 78th day, morning session.

I am introduced. I come to the box as a witness.

The presiding judge starts out a little harshly. He won't insult me—he barely bothers to say hello!—by announcing this session as if it is a recess in this marathon trial that "we" have experienced for two and a half months now.

He won't insult me ... however, I feel insulted (I'm exaggerating a little) and I tell him so. I thank the judge in the proper fashion, adding that, in rhetoric, what he has committed is called a paraleipsis.

A good loser, the presiding judge agrees. His disposition quickly regains the upper hand. The judge doesn't mince words. That would be one more reason not to stall.

I don't see why he needs one more reason. Hurry through, Your Honor! But who told him that I won't take two days? Or three?

The presiding judge is annoyed. Anything is possible. Isn't there a benevolent lawyer here to drop the word into the whorl of my ear that a trial is a serious thing and will not be reduced to a private barroom chat between a judge and an accused ... uh ... a witness? He made this slip—

I'm making up nothing.

One of the lawyers for the defense asks for the floor while apologizing and taking it. He points out the fact that the broaching of the subject by the presiding judge was . . . if he could be so bold . . . a little cavalier, although quite understandable after the marathon that has been imposed on everyone by circumstances. He says that his client admits to a little fatigue (his great age), that he cannot be reproached with not taking an interest in the debate (unlike certain parties) and that one day of respite wouldn't be extravagant.

So, when are they going to get to me?

After a murderous glance at the bench of the accused, the presiding judge responds that it shouldn't be any more tiring than to preside over the interminable meetings of the Chamber of Deputies. In effect, the team of the accused isn't looking that great. Their appearance is dull. This is perhaps because, as everyone knows, these faces are generally seen only through makeup. The judge again says all right and calls for seriousness. I am about to ask who first lacked seriousness but change my mind the moment he turns toward me. Stéphane, is that indeed my surname? and my first name, then?

There isn't a first name.

Have I signed my X? Am I ready to solemnly swear the habitual oaths? Nothing but the, the whole . . .

Certainly. I swear it. And I don't swear in an offhand manner. I become solemn.

The presiding judge continues asking for trouble. Is that not too difficult a thing for a novelist to swear to tell the truth? Occupation: novelist, that's it, right?

I say, a little dryly, that a novelist—not only novelist, writer!—who respects himself swears to it each morning before his piece of paper, or before his computer screen, at least on one condition.

Which one?

On the condition that he works in the morning! The spectators laugh. The presiding judge is ruffled but he doesn't take it badly. The atmosphere becomes a bit more relaxed.

As if he were tempted by the prospect of a joust, the judge asks me if I know that, sometimes, the state of being a witness and that of being a defendant are separated from each other by the thinness of cigarette paper . . .

I answer that I don't smoke, Your Honor . . . but I think that, if I did, I would roll my own, actually. This time, I make no one laugh other than the judge himself. His laughter is a little forced. He is the sort of man who entirely dominates his laughter, makes it rise to just where he wants it and cuts it off instantly . . . I tell myself I would do better to hold my tongue.

The presiding judge wants to get on with the interrogation. He surrenders the floor to the public prosecutor, who had asked for it.

The attorney leads off with a specious assertion followed by a harmless question. It's a classic. The trap is to respond right away to the question without disputing the assertion. I had been in close contact with certain of the accused. Can I say in what circumstances?

I have never been in close contact with certain of the accused. They granted me interviews, never without witnesses. Now . . . I try to pronounce the following phrase without looking at the principal defendant. At the time of the announcement, ten years ago, by the government of the Republic, of the great Mountain R project, I for my part shared, with the presidency of the Republican Council, in writing, my intention of composing a work of fiction which would borrow its material (all its material, nothing but its material) from the conception and realization of the project. This intention had the excellent fortune of pleasing the highest authorities.

The public prosecutor tells me with a certain sourness that I am not obligated to recite it as if it were one of La Fontaine's fables.

I say that it is not in *that* manner that I recite the fables of La Fontaine, but that I have already made this declaration at least twenty times since I have been questioned . . . no, since I have been *harassed* about this matter.

Without rising, the public prosecutor asks me in what fashion then did the authorities express this enthusiasm?

Why . . . in the exorbitant sum of the monetary advance that was granted to me. Only infectious enthusiasm can give rise to that!

Ah, there! Let's go back a little . . . I had met, in the days which followed my missive, the president of the Republican Council of that time. He gave me the green light, as well as a comfortable advance, which was moreover voted on, according to the rules, by the ad hoc commission. I preserved, of course, all my rights concerning the text to come. I feel that it is up to me to utter aloud and distinctly the total of the amount. That will have less of a negative effect on the spectators than if it is thrown in my face. This grant amounted to an annuity of 300,000 francs, tacitly understood to be renewable for six years (thus seven total annuities). That corresponded with, at the time, the presumed duration of the construction. In the most professional tone I can muster, I add that it was a fine contract.

The attorney for the Republic has a scowl of disdain, as if the money came out of his own pocket. Let's stay on topic. I had never invested a centime of this amount in the stocks (once rather popular) of Mountain R. Should this be seen as a sign of mistrust of the project? Wasn't I haughtily "biting the hand that feeds me," as the saying goes? Why hadn't I taken part in the promotional campaigns for the purchase of these stocks along with an appreciable number of celebrities of the arts, letters, and the stage?

I answer too quickly. I am forced to. My answer: very simply because I was by no means a profitable celebrity. Nobody solicited me in this way.

Was that to say then, if I had been a "profitable" celebrity, I would have composed without scruple an *Ode to Mountain R Stock?*

Nicely played, the allusion. Let's say that in this case I would certainly have been asked.

Would I have resisted?

To accept would have been contrary to the discretion of my project. Furthermore, I was never in the habit of purchasing stock. I wouldn't have *resisted,* I would have *declined.*

Easy to say. I hadn't applied either, as so many other sycophants of this accursed construction project, for an apartment on the future slopes.

No.

Why?

I am a perpetual renter.

My interrogator announces to me—some revelation!— that nearly ten years have passed since this attractive contract, and that construction has since stopped. He believes he knows that my annual payments were suspended by the parliamentary commission eighteen months ago (it had thus been paid to me for eight years, not seven), which is perfectly true, and I declare as much, and I say without bitterness that the House had the power to stop the payments by virtue of the contract itself, which had become null and void since the construction had come to a standstill.

What have I lived on since that time?

Why . . . I live in other ways. I am devoting myself to a biography of Eugène de Mirecourt, a rather strange character, who hunted for lice on Alexandre Dumas's head, lice to which the celebrated novelist planned to give jobs. Can you imagine!

The public prosecutor can't imagine. Or does so badly. It seems that I am steering my boat well.

What does he mean by that?

Haven't I dug up a new comfortable grant for this biography?

Yes, from a private organization.

Which?

Bouin Bank.

I hear my name at the start of a sentence that intends to be menacing: Mr Stéphane . . . if I am not here on the bench of the accused, it is simply because we are in cramped quarters. There is no other reason. If there had been only four more places on the bench—he indicates the bench of the accused—that's where I'd be sitting. It's funny: the accused threw a glance at the little space they had between them on the bench, as if they wanted to make a little room for me. The preliminary investigation didn't judge it proper to pursue. Am I aware of this?

Oh! certainly, I am aware of it . . . That had been made quite clear to me!

The public prosecutor is surprised at my sudden humility.

He can't know—it has nothing to do with him!—that for some time I have depleted the greater part of my strength in a great . . . shall we say, sadness, and that at least today I will not have a lot of time to think about her. I will perhaps look a little better because of that. I turn myself toward the presiding judge and respectfully ask him to reassure me: all the same I wouldn't have been a primary defendant?

That's because writers have always been the Republic's darlings!

Excuse me?

The presiding judge remains impassive, as if he had not heard my short protest. He lets the public prosecutor answer. I would have been one of the less significant of those charged on the 78th day . . . The accused, here, were truly a rare commodity! I had said, at the time of the preliminary investigation, that I had met the #1 defendant rather easily. How did I go about it? Hurrah for changing the subject. The question stings me.

I don't hesitate very long. I say that, in the simplest way possible, I had asked for a meeting. I wasn't the only one.

And I had gotten it, just like that? . . . The public prosecutor snaps his fingers. Some people didn't get one.

Just like that, yes. The president made me aware that my name wasn't unknown to him. I hadn't brought any influence into play.

How did this idea come to me, to follow this construction project in the manner of a chronicler? Would that be an accurate description of my role, a "chronicler"?

With that, I returned to familiar ground. It was the moment to show off a little. I answered clearly: No. I didn't want to write a chronicle, but rather a novel. It would have been my ninth novel. I had no idea of the way in which this novel would incorporate observed reality. What had fascinated me, in the announcement of this extraordinary thing, Mountain R, was precisely the likeness that I found in it to my experience as a novelist. To write a novel is to be obligated, just like that, to build a mountain from scratch on a lot adjacent to your own. You see it progress every day from your window. Every day, without consideration for vacations or days off. A mountain next to your life. You must count the pages, estimate the number of words, portion out the chapters. A certain fine accumulation . . . the rough product underneath, and the more one rises toward the surface, the more elaborate it is . . . Each word must be as shaped as every other, each sentence carefully articulated within the whole. One knows that this will demand several months, sometimes several years, of loving effort . . . If one dies in the middle, nobody will finish the project. One has to be a worker like Balzac.

The presiding judge asked me if I was accustomed to using this sort of writing process with my other novels.

I asked if reading my novels had been part of the work of the examining magistrate. But I was made to understand that I was not to pose perfidious questions. So I said, Not at all. This process wasn't customary for me.

I had rather a reputation for being a cerebral writer. Hadn't I been surprised to obtain the contract so easily? Hadn't I obtained this wonderful contract by a misunderstanding? The odds were that I wouldn't have delivered an epic that would have, with emotion, spoken to the heart of the masses!

I thanked the attorney for these kind words. I had obtained this contract because my previous book had been particularly admired by some of my fellow artists—and not the least among them—who had made their appreciation known. That hadn't made me any more "popular," but put me on certain lists.

What book were we talking about?

Late Disclosures on What Really Happened in the Cockpit.

A novel?

Of course.

On what?

Paper.

There was glacial silence.

If my interrogator understood properly, I was fascinated by the decision of a lone man to build a mountain, a man whose megalomaniac characteristics no longer needed to be proven. Was I too as megalomanic as he?

At the very most I would have *in that case* been fascinated, I corrected. But at that moment Mountain R was a national project. The House had approved it. Opinion wasn't neutral. The media spoke ironically while secretly rubbing their hands (finally, an event!) and while inundating their pages and television screens with prognostications and controversies. The banks did as they were told. There was a very deep breath taken as money was swallowed up. I had got my share of the loot.

Had I said *loot?*

I didn't notice. I wanted this novel to espouse a collective passion. I knew I was taking a risk.

The word "risk" seemed to plunge the public prosecutor into the foulest incomprehension. Of what nature, this *risk?*

Let's say that the only real risk was that the novel would never get finished. That's precisely what happened.

Disappointed?

Accustomed.

Was I able to avoid answering in one word sentences?

For one novel that comes to fruition, five others are dead ends.

I could have made a successful novel out of an aborted mountain . . . from a Mountain R as in *Ruined!*

Impossible. For me, impossible.

I had stopped my work well before knowing that the construction wouldn't reach its end!

Yes. It wasn't stipulated in the contract that I absolutely had to finish it.

I needed to tell them a little about my work, without being afraid of giving details. There was time.

My intention was . . . hmmm . . . how to go about it? I believe that we are in a society where it is necessary for us to protect information. Everyone is too informed . . . In seeing the frowns the press bench was making, I put a little water into my wine: when I say that everyone is too informed, I mean to say, obviously, too poorly informed . . . Everyone faces this pile of information that is difficult to sort out . . . And who is responsible for promoting the idea that the media enjoys this kind of exorbitant power? The media itself! Obviously the press must do its job . . . of course they were hindered from doing it during the construction of Mountain R, and it was disastrous . . . but, too often, problems are exposed to the full light of day only when a solution is already lurking in the shadows. I wanted, for once in my life, to find myself upstream, to have access to the original spring and to see what was welling up in it, in fictional terms. It was in wanting a "permanent pass" that I had solicited the president of the Council, making quite clear I wouldn't be satisfied with partial access. It was necessary for me to be able to be where I wanted, when I wanted. This interested the president so much that he asked me right away to come chatter with him each week, once I had started. He had used the word "chatter."

And why, in my opinion?

Why the word?

Why the invitation!

I answered, a little bit too tit-for-tat, that now (or never) was the moment to ask *him* . . .

Then it was the presiding judge who began to speak, irritated that the impossible thing against which he had been colliding for more than two months had come up again. Was I unaware, I who was so well informed, that the #1 defendant was being absolutely silent after having spoken out so often when he was in power? On his bench, the interested party kept his eyes closed, without any apparent tension, which was rather impressive. He was not threatened by death. He tried to make himself forgotten. He'd succeeded very well. One could argue for an hour without thinking of him. I hadn't answered the preceding question.

The response was so simple that I formulated it without conviction: he could never have too many spies. But I had declined those invitations to spy. They indicated all too well that my project wasn't understood. Besides, it hadn't been of importance. A writer can work all his life without being very well understood . . . Being understood well is not necessarily a virtue, but it isn't a vice either.

The accused . . .

He hadn't aged. Lost weight, yes. I had not seen the president of the Republican Council in person again until this day.

It was granted that that was effectively more or less attested to. The accused . . . but then the prosecutor changed ground. I did not, however, keep myself from launching forth in the day's newspapers (not just any, the most subservient to those in power at the time) to intone—just in case— the epic of Mountain R.

Ouch!

A certain "Ode to Bargeco" didn't exactly shimmer with subtlety . . . Besides, it was observed that it didn't figure into the collection of my poems that had just appeared . . . otherwise rather complete, according to the specialists. Would I assert that the "Ode to Bargeco" hadn't been worth, from this colossus of public works, a few emoluments coming to add themselves to my already comfortable grant from the State?

This confounded "Ode to Bargeco," how many times had I been reproached for it?

Not-a-cent-ime! I syllabated with firmness. I asked that they put themselves in my place . . .

And then what?

Anyone who was placed in this situation would have quickly learned that it was necessary to win the confidence of Bargeco or else stay behind barbed wire (on this side) with the scrap of presidential paper that would make no difference whatever to the gangs of watchmen. And yes, despite the discretionary power that short-sighted minds attribute to a lone man . . . a truly solitary man doesn't exist. Ever. So, I backed up my presidential favor with that of Bargeco: back to front. Consequently, I was bulletproof.

This manner, in the interrogations, of recording the answer as if it had no power of conviction! And this manner of shooting a new arrow towards an apparently completely different target! At the time of this beautiful . . . shall we say ideological admiration of Mountain R, in what amount of time did I imagine delivering my novel to the public?

Always the same trap of the debatable assertion followed by a simple question. I never felt the least shadow of an ideological admiration for that undertaking . . . There was in the assembly a rumbling of ridicule, which hurt me. I know that they had distributed, that same morning, an extract from the "Ode to Bargeco" at the entrance to the courts, a one-page double-sided flyer. Sympathetic fellow artists, no doubt.

Did I want them just to quote for me a few lines from "Ode to Bargeco," lines that appeared twice in the weekly papers of the time? Perhaps I hadn't kept a single copy in my archives? It must be pleasant for a poet to hear his lines read in public in a hall covered in paneling, with perfect acoustics.

I didn't condescend to answer.

It is the presiding judge who is bent on reading them to me. Reading them *for us*. He reads overdramatically, obviously.

[...]

the man is before the main route, leaning against his truck
if he stretches his arms, behold the new man of Vitrivius
you don't sense the man of woe beaten back into shape
the man and his enterprise will give birth to a Vesuvius
[...]

He said: it's all like that!

The courtroom audience broke out in laughter.

Do I disown these lines?

I argued that these lines were inevitable. They would have been replaced in . . . They weren't any worse than many others. Poetry is not something purer than anything

112

else, nor less corrupt.

"Man" in each line, didn't that grate on me? Must have been intentional. And "Vesuvius," when all around Mountain R so many deaths had been counted up?

I only knew to answer by asking if I were a witness or a prisoner. Silence from in front of me.

The CEO of Bargeco . . . rather the ex-, once again . . . Madame Lalande-Plumet . . . here present . . . you were close, no?

How to know what they knew? They had already interrogated her, but how to know what she had told them? I had prepared nothing. Madame Lalande-Plumet took a lot of interest in literature. In her day, she had translated Italian and Romanian poets. Thus, she didn't hate it when I spoke to her about literature. Nothing more. She had nothing to do with getting me my contract.

Really? Hadn't I met her again in Bologna at a conference of urban planners?

If Mountain R hadn't been at the heart of conferences of urban planners in those years, I wonder what would have been!

Yes, but you were a couple . . .

Certainly not, we were friends at a conference, that's all . . .

. . . manner of speaking . . . wasn't continually in session, that's the least that could be said. It was enough that they examined the minutes of the conference. They had examined them.

But no . . . nothing at all.

The presiding judge asked that we back up a little, so as to move things forward, to what he called my "method." He asserted that it wasn't lacking in interest. And then, I had not responded about the delay in publication.

Publication? But . . . it was to be published the day of Mountain R's inauguration! Which is to say—never! As for the interest shown in my method . . . I had really stopped being conscious of it. And I said so. My method was awkward and sterile. I could make nothing of the various things I'd seen. Already while picking apart the press reports one is quickly flooded with confusion . . . But there, it was still worse, that was what surprised me the most. I wasn't expecting it. I had naively hoped for the opposite. It would have been better for me to make things up.

Could I explain all that in detail? . . . Since we were finally getting at things I could be blamed for: refusal to surrender my information, after my project had run aground . . .

I reaffirmed that I had preserved nothing. This kind of material is eminently perishable. If it didn't help, you had to get rid of it. Otherwise, it's poison for the projects that take its place.

How can I be believed?

I recalled that ten thorough searches had yielded nothing.

I might well have managed to put some papers in a secure place. A writer who burns his manuscripts is unheard of, since the market value of them was considerable today, at least potentially in my case.

I am, however, of those who burn. I preserved nothing.

The manuscripts, they didn't care much about those . . . what they wanted were the documents.

But what documents? My clearance didn't authorize me to photocopy the confidential files!

But I indeed went to the project meetings! I attended meetings . . .

At the beginning, yes. But it was too trying a task. Trying or boring. And then, they looked askance at me . . . They multiplied the technical terms and the slang of the profession, so that I couldn't understand . . .

I didn't understand anything?

Of the details, little. That's true. But I indeed saw . . . how to say it? On the slopes of Mountain R, each time one lifted a new file, each time one lifted a new clod, a lot of trouble (and troublemakers) started to emerge. It is like that in all moments of history when established jurisidictions find themselves suddenly maladjusted, and when everything seems almost possible. New actions collide with obsolete regulations. Then comes the reign of might and of "special dispensation." Mountain R leveled a lot of things. It would have perhaps changed republican society more profoundly than many revolutions. But it's true . . . as soon as I realized that the construction site of Mountain R was the privileged locus of modern *slavery* (intentional stress on slavery), I interrupted my work, and in an irrevocable manner. If I had continued, I would have had no other recourse but to denounce what I had caught a glimpse of.

That wouldn't have hurt my reputation! Didn't I believe that novelists, that intellectuals, had straightforward political responsibilities in the domain of ideas?

Hog-butchers, too, have the right to have ideas, and by consequence responsibilities in the domain of ideas. There were hog-butchers who delivered sausages to the Bargeco canteen. They knew perhaps as much as I. Have you summoned them? Ideas are things too serious to be seen as entrusted to mere specialists. The courtroom didn't like my rejoinder, which seemed cowardly.

Had I had the feeling of acting in a blameworthy manner? Of being ungrateful?

One will grant me simply that it would have been dangerous to speak out. Further, nobody would have wanted to believe me. I had no authority in the matter. My prior works hadn't in any way prepared for it. You can't teach a nation with one eye missing and the other eye blinded, following a leader blind from birth, by punching it in the face. Look at the story of Kurt Gerstein. Besides, "literature must never serve as a testimony." Call it my own Hippocratic oath, or my dirty secret.

There were a hundred examples in which literature had served as a witness. What was unworthy about that? Hadn't I ever read Voltaire or Zola? Or Gide? Didn't I feel as if I were killing Semes Yamin again, he who denounced the working conditions of his compatriots, and then was assassinated—ostensibly at least—by the Kurds?

When one speaks of a "political inspiration" for a writer, the politics of reference are always the school of hard knocks! Me, I'm sorry, but I take an interest in *soft* knocks. I was willing to be accountable to the present moment, but I must also be accountable to history as well, to the history, especially, of my art, and those two responsibilities can find themselves at odds.

How did destroying this testimony (assuming I had destroyed it), how did hiding this testimony move in the direction of a larger responsibility to history? That was beyond them.

I said that a writer acts through a book, not through a cock-and-bull story disguised as literature, pretending to be literature. I didn't succeed with the book. I had a formal ambition, and I was overwhelmed by the conceit. To write is not to foresee. Don't confuse the two. Obviously, I made a mistake. I would have had to choose as an event the most miniscule thing possible: the construction of a garden shed or of a Swiss cuckoo clock, not a mountain ... I found myself in the position of an architect who dreams of being Le Nôtre or Frank Lloyd Wright and who realizes that his profession consists of plugging holes and of juggling standards and regulations.

All that was only of passing interest. The public prosecutor looked as if he regretted that I hadn't been indicted for failing to assist people in danger, and for complicity in a crime against humanity.

That wasn't a question.

It remains that, at the time, I would have been able to give the press firsthand information. It remains that, even if I hadn't wanted to, for want of the most elementary courage ...

But to be precise, it is cowardice that is elementary!

... courage to put my hands in directly, I would have been able to establish contact with the opposition. There weren't many, but all the same! I knew enough people!

I didn't answer.

Let's assume that I had preserved nothing in writing ... In all the interviews that I had had with the major players of Mountain R, I had perhaps made a few recordings?

I said that I didn't much like to work with a tape recorder. To listen to the tapes again is too boring, and then attention to the moment tends to fade: you no longer trust your memory. I don't have a tape recorder.

If however I was summoned to testify, I could say things by word of mouth . . . I saw nothing to prevent me from . . . ?

Of course not . . . naturally . . . I could tell of the spreading of the first sack of dirt when, in the center of a large and quite regal terreplein, at zero feet above sea level (in fact, it was cheating, they were in the large ditch surrounding the construction site which would be considered *sea level* once they had finished clearing all the dirt away), the president dumped a big sack of dirt which made a ridiculous little pyramid.

If only I had pronounced the word *ridiculous* sooner! Further, I taught them nothing about that day. There was nothing particularly secret about it. Enough filmic documents, photographs . . . why didn't I tell instead of the day of the famous memory lapse?

Which one? It's true that there were many of them, but I knew very well that they wanted to talk about the one most written about: the day that the president of the Republican Council should have gone to the construction site for a heaven-sent opportunity. An acknowledgable accident that time, that's to say, acknowledgable because inevitable: lightning had struck a crew of electricians. Natural disaster equals innocence. Innocence in politics equals benefit for personal image. One renders homage to the actors of the drama, without realizing that among the actors is thunder!

Three dead, two seriously burned, saved by the composure of a young immigrant. The president . . .

I should force myself to say "ex-"

At the time he wasn't ex-! Very well, the *ex*-president had said, thinking to cut short rumors about a string of accidents (the earlier ones more murderous), had said, concerning the electricians: "We went to salute the bodies. There were three. We saw the bodies firsthand." It was horrible. Yes, I was there. The president, the ex-, took me for a witness. He no longer remembered my name, he called me "Mr Christian." He literally dragged me before the throng of cameras and asked me to tell all that I knew about the great progress of the construction project. He said "about the optimum progress!" And that I was the one most in a position to give this indisputable information . . . I was horribly embarrassed.

Right then, the presiding judge asked to view the film.

Wait . . . was I, once again, witness or accused? I repeated that because I was beginning to get worried.

It wasn't to see me, but the ex-!

I had forgotten how much I had stammered in front of the camera, not daring to cause a scandal. In any case, even if I had caused a scandal, it wasn't a live broadcast, it would never have been transmitted. In fact, it wasn't transmitted then, either. The ex-president was much too charged up. I didn't see why this film, which stayed in its canister, would have been produced for the indictment of anybody!

Did I want to excuse the #1 defendant?

That's not what I wanted to say. The #1 accused, during the projection, had looked at the screen without the least trace of emotion.

In the course of my visits at the start of construction, had I seen at work brigades of drafted soldiers surrounded by armed guards and assault dogs?

I had seen brigades, but I didn't know it was a question of drafted soldiers. I hadn't for one second imagined that. They were presented by Bargeco as common criminals who were in this way purchasing their future liberation. Yes, I had been able to question one of them. To ask if he was paid. He told me yes, of course. He seemed to be in good health. But my memory of him is rather vague. I wouldn't recognize him, no. I have already been asked that ten times; I have been shown hundreds of photographs, I never knew his name. I have already said that despite the best intentions in the world I couldn't help the Association of Parents of the Vanished, who are looking for their sons. I didn't keep a single piece of information in my possession.

Obviously I had not preserved a single note, a single notebook . . . I didn't keep a personal journal . . .

No, nothing, I destroyed everything, bits of illegible paper . . . I have already said it a thousand times. You must believe me.

Had I written any correspondent to tell him what I saw? . . .

No, not one. I was already writing all day long . . . as if it were still necessary to write letters!

Had I been happy with the choice of architect? I had indeed participated in the deliberations of the jury who were supposed to close the competition.

The jury was a joke. Everybody knew it. Everyone was already saying it at the time. The project chosen was the tackiest . . . at first sight the quickest to put into operation, that was the principle reason for its success. Personally, I was for Jacques Deneux's project, but it was too utopian. He wanted, first of all, to make the mountain from foam, in order to ensure the plasticity of its material . . . A lot less expensive . . . with systems of honeycombs . . . and really slippery parts . . . but he excused himself from the competition upon seeing to what degree it was rigged. That was when he put forward the idea of a hologram. There were extraordinary projects: a mountain in snow . . . entirely raised by snow blowers . . . melted each summer, recreated each winter . . . I no longer know who authored that project . . . There was also the purely conceptual hypothesis (Ignazi plan): it was enough that Mountain R have a strong silhouette, like Cervin or Ventoux, like Fujiyama, and that it be available on t-shirts, ashtrays, and stickers . . . its synthesized image could occupy all the screens

of the world . . . But that was the work of amiable uto-
pians. They weren't in the majority. They didn't stand a
chance.

Instead I should speak of the others. Wasn't it too tiring,
for morale, to meet so many greedy people?

I hadn't met only villains, far from it! During the years
of Mountain R, why shouldn't there be honest profession-
als acting in good faith? They existed. I had met them in
equal proportion to their opposite, and in all the subordinate
positions where wage-earners don't ask themselves about
the origin or the smell of the money paid them. That was
the case for a certain engineer. And for a certain geologist,
and for other foremen.

I had to give names.

Certainly not! I spoke of an impression of the whole . . .
To justify the Republic, one further blackens this bad period
. . . But so what? It was hard, perhaps rightly . . . but you
know, for those who lived on this construction site, near or
far . . . for those who lived on this construction site . . . it was
very livable! With that, I created an uproar.

Had I seen children work?

Children, no, young adolescents, yes.

What age?

Difficult to say . . . sixteen . . . children are so big today
. . .

Did I suppose that the utilization of refuse and residue,

domestic and industrial, in the great landfill could have had its equivalent in the domain of manpower: to empty troubled towns of their youngest revolutionaries?

I had for a long time rejected this idea.

But I should have accepted it, yes or no?

Yes.

After the incident of the lightning and the crew of electricians, I left for the United States?

Exactly.

I had continued to collect my annual endowment, although I was no longer working on my project at all?

Yes, I had sent a registered letter to the department which disbursed this grant informing them that I unilaterally canceled my contract. But, inexplicably, the money had continued to be deposited into my account. At first, I had set it aside to give back upon my possible return.

And then, I had had a pressing need for it when I had made friends with Miss Muratore . . .

All this was true.

With that, and very curtly, as if he had waited for these words since morning, the presiding judge said that the session was adjourned until two o'clock.

*

*   *

It is still the 78th day, afternoon session. I am reintroduced.

As one finds one's bearings . . . The presiding judge decides that we haven't gotten very far.

I said that I wasn't the timekeeper for the court.

The public prosecutor had a little difficulty speaking, as if he had eaten too much and too quickly. This money, nobody had required in advance that I must return it if it so happened that I didn't write the novel . . . The contract did not formally stipulate any delivery of a finished product. That was lucky for me. I couldn't be accused of embezzlement . . .

What he had said I had, in effect, set myself up for. Further, it wasn't a question. I didn't have to respond.

How had I met Miss Muratore?

At a party in Boston.

Someone introduced us to one another?

No. She had been in a corner since the start of the reception. She was bored. She had a vaguely hurt look. So, quite simply, I spoke to her. A half-hour later, we spoke of Mountain R. It was a coincidence. We both had something to do with Mountain R.

By that time, however, I had completely abandoned my project . . .

Yes, completely, but the Mountain reclaimed me. It was rather disagreeable. But, *a contrario,* my new friend, she was very agreeable. There was an ample balance.

Who, of she and I, had first spoken of Mountain R?

I don't remember. When one spoke of the Republic at that time, it was difficult not to point the conversation towards Mountain R. It was obvious right away, however, that we were both Republicans.

What was Miss Muratore doing in Boston?

She herself wondered as much.

What was *I* doing in Boston?

I was trying to forget Mountain R.

By speaking about it with the first person to come along? . . . What did Miss Muratore have to do with Mountain R?

The most absurd news had started to leak out about the project. Most was true, as you are in the process of establishing. The daughter of Muratore asked herself questions about how her father, who you know better at present than she did then, spent his time.

How many years of difference in age were there between Miss Muratore and myself?

Thirty.

In what way were we *together*?

We didn't live together, but we spoke every day without exception, in person or on the telephone. It was a tender relationship, which perhaps was not meant to last any longer than it did. It gave me a jolt of love, by saying which I mean a jolt of heat but of little hope.

Since the suicide of Muratore, the father, I had never seen my friend again?

Never.

Had I known this Muratore?

I had heard *of* him.

Around the construction site?

Yes.

In what terms?

Odious ones.

By whom?

Pragesse.

Jean Pragesse?

Of course.

Who said what to me?

As far as I could understand ... because he spoke with difficulty, this boy ... he above all spoke highly of him. He admired him like a lost boy admires a gang leader lacking all scruples. Violent, crude, selfish.

Under what conditions had I been able to meet Pragesse?

He was one of the most media-hyped faces of Mountain R.

Did I think that Jean Pragesse could have been executed by Muratore?

I have no idea.

Is it a completely preposterous possibility?

127

No, I wouldn't say so.

At the time of his seventh interrogation, the next-to-last before his suicide, Muratore asserted that his daughter came to ask him lots of questions because she worked for an American firm interested in the technique and the hazards of the project. Wasn't this American firm not simply me? Didn't I continue to accumulate documentation on Mountain R?

She must surely have told you that she didn't know what to think of her father . . . They had between them a sort of moat of misrecognition. For her, for her peace of mind, it was necessary that she fill this moat in. Certain people have too much past, others not enough. She didn't have enough. I convinced her to go look for information at the source, by actively making up this story of working for an American firm, a story which seemed to me sufficiently likely to put to bed the mistrust that I imagined would come from Muratore.

She must surely have reported this information to me?

That wasn't at all required.

She reported it to me, yes or no?

Yes. She reported it to me. But I don't know if she reported all of it. It didn't matter. The important thing was that she gathered this information, not that she pass it on to me.

Did I therefore have a reason for sending this young lady on a, at very least, delicate investigation? After all, I was the one who had financed her trip to the Republic!

But . . . I don't want to speak of that in front of everybody!

I seemed troubled by the question.

It was private.

The response of Miss Muratore, which she had pronounced without qualm at the time of the preliminary investigation, was that I had a project for her . . .

That *we* had a project *together!*

. . . that I had a project for her, that's what she said. Could I say what it was? She didn't seem as engaged in this project as I had believed and hoped.

We contemplated, together, an expedition to the North Pole.

Why did she want to go to the Pole?

Silence from me.

Miss Muratore had no particular reason to go to the Pole. I was the one who had superficially imposed it, because I wanted to write a historical novel about the voyage of Pierre Louis Moreau de Maupertuis, who left Lapland to measure the arc of the meridian closest to the arctic circle, thus demonstrating the hypothesis (expressed by Huygens) of the flattening out of the earth near the poles. This voyage took place in 1736-37.

It wasn't necessary to recite it like a prayer!

I had the intention of going farther than Maupertuis, did I not? As far as the Pole?

I didn't know what to say, either for or against. Or even round about.

What was I expecting from the Pole? Did I have a scientific motive?

I recited within myself a saying out of Maupertius which had really captured our imaginations: "Up to us to be stubborn, to put to the test the horrors of winter in the frigid zone . . . " Me, I wanted to write a novel, a scientific enough thing.

Had I obtained the grant that I had requested from the Warren Motte Foundation for the trip and for the writing of the novel?

It was, at that time, looking good.

No doubt it would be. In what way would Miss Muratore have been better equipped for this journey to the Pole after having squeezed secrets out of her father?

Introductory Psychology. Not better equipped . . . unencumbered.

Did she have a mission to convince her father to give her money which would have given my project a boost.

Our project. But . . . not in any way!

However, Muratore had well and truly given her the money. That's what he had asserted. That's what she had acknowledged. This gift was moreover perfectly legal, the inheritance fees had been settled beforehand. There was nothing to be objected to.

But I was unaware of it.

Yes, because this money stayed in the Republic. Before her lightning-quick trip to the Republic, had I communicated what I knew of the "odious" reputation of Muratore, of which I had spoken a little bit earlier?

No. She needed to learn it from his mouth, not from mine.

I hadn't told her that the name of Muratore was not unknown to me?

No, I hadn't told her.

But wasn't my silence explicit in itself?

Possibly.

She would then have learned the details from the justice system.

Yes.

Was I by now aware of everything the law had since revealed?

The proceedings hadn't yet been published, had they? I had read the news rather regularly.

Did I know that Muratore organized the rounding up of idle youths so as to swell the decimated ranks of Ukrainian workers? Or perhaps for something worse . . .

I suspected that this "rounding up," as he called it, took

place. I believed the numbers to be low. A few zealous dog-catchers with a big net, like in the cartoons. I didn't have any proof.

Did I know that Muratore backed up this official job with a prostitution ring, this time with female minors from the same districts?

I didn't know that.

Hadn't I asked myself about the sexual activities in a construction project of that size (a thousand males) and of that duration, so cut off from the rest of the world?

Yes, as one asks such questions about prisons, about barracks . . . But I was neither a sociologist nor a journalist.

Had I never attended one of those sinister parties that provided bodies for the north side? Hadn't I, too, shot a rifle with a scope on the slopes of Mountain R? Wasn't my name on one of the lists of these hunts?

Invited, yes, and I was perhaps still in the index file, as a result of my special clearance. But I had never gone.

I wasn't without knowledge that the ex-president of the Republican Council was a great hunter. The photo of his living room with all his trophies had often been published . . .

Yes, I knew.

Hadn't I, myself, hunted with my father during childhood, and until the age of 22?

Certainly, I was the one who furnished this information quite a long time ago . . . Only I . . . I'd stopped hunting when I was old enough to understand how they scared up game.

Then, had I hunted, yes or no, on the slopes of Mountain R, as the majority of the dignitaries of the regime had done?

No. But hadn't it been testified to that these parties had taken place in the last two years of construction, well after my departure for the United States? I had never been a dignitary of the regime.

Testified to that the parties had taken place the last two years, yes. But that didn't mean there hadn't been others beforehand.

Me, I didn't know.

Did I know what kind of game was hunted?

I had just learned.

What kind?

At first animal game was released . . . then wounded or ineffectual workers.

How many?

Nobody knows.

Fifteen attested to, killed by bullets. They weren't going to take down the whole mountain to make certain that there weren't other mass graves! The Mountain had already cost enough. It wouldn't be touched any more until further notice. It would be left to settle. Unless I might really want to finish my novel and, with my small savings, undertake to finance excavations?

I didn't respond to this provocation.

Did I know why the camps of the Turks, the Ukrainians, and, later, the Hutus, had been situated on the least stable side of Mountain R?

Obviously because it was the most discreet, the most remote from official paths . . . Everyone understood this. You didn't need to be on familiar terms with the Bargeco staff to know that!

Had I known Valérie Marneffe?

No.

Had I known ex-Colonel Mazars?

I hadn't known him.

Did I have anything to say about the scandal known as 'artificial snow,' in which all of the underground pipes and couplings had been bought from a phony company, and the materials never delivered?

So what?

Did I know that, with the financial gulf deepening, the share of the State in the assets of the MRC made it the controlling shareholder at the price of a phenomenal national debt?

Inevitably! I knew also that the bankruptcy of Mountain R hadn't stopped the banks from recording handsome profits. By the way . . . I was surprised not to find their managing directors on the bench of the accused.

I was not the examining magistrate, nor the attorney for the Republic.

That's true.

Did I know something about the so-called activity of information services hired by our neighbors, which would have impeded the progress of the construction project?

So-called seemed to me to be the right word. The progress of the construction project had been impeded by the enormity of the task.

That was, in my opinion, the decisive reason?

Yes. Added to finances, obviously . . . the exorbitant cost of the enormous task. Perhaps a bad solution had been chosen. A more conceptual solution would have been more reliable. You could have made a single side, facing fully south, mounted on a framework. It was one of the proposals . . .

But that didn't settle the problem of the view from behind, nor of life under the framework.

That could have been explored . . .

Had I really never met ex-Deputy Bouton walking with his dogs, a gun slung over his arm? He had nevertheless cited me in the middle of a long list of distinguished people who expressed their unconditional admiration for this uncommon construction project.

I asked if his word as an accused was as good as mine.

On his bench, Bouton seemed crushed. He didn't want to pay attention to me. He stared at a point on the ground between his feet. Now and then he closed an eye, as if he were going to take a photo or conduct a monocular optical experiment.

At this moment, one of the lawyers for the defense expressed a relative protest as to my inability to bring even the least supporting light to the accusations as a whole. He insinuated that everyone's time was being wasted. Which angered the public prosecutor, who suddenly produced a dispatch that had just reached him. In a nice flight of oratory, he exclaimed that Mountain R had just struck anew. Not later than this morning, idle youths had gone to ride motorbikes on the slopes, in spite of the prohibition. They had been attacked by a mob of vagrants who had taken shelter in the abandoned hangers on the summit. It was possible that they were the former Bargeco watchmen. Three of these youths had been injured by stones thrown at them. Another was reported missing! Were the authorities going to have to attack them? To drop battalions of paratroopers onto this stump of a mountain?

The proceedings seemed to want to move away from my personal circumstances . . . But they soon came back to them, without great conviction. Perhaps I had underestimated the seriousness of the case history of Muratore, the father? . . .

It's a good assumption.

If I had perfectly understood the situation, would I have pushed my friend into that investigation?

Impossible to respond to such a question.

Did I believe that it was necessary to know everything about one's family history?

If one couldn't tolerate the lack of knowledge, one must do all that one can to discover the truth, whatever there is to be discovered.

When I had again met my friend after her conversation with her father, what had she told me, exactly?

She was a little stunned, because the police had taken her father away before her very eyes. She had had to take care of the dog, put it in a kennel . . .

I didn't answer the question. What had she told me?

She didn't want to tell me anything. Except that, speaking of construction, of the duration of construction, her father tapped his fingernail on the marble tabletop to indicate the accumulation of days. Except that the old man was short of breath, and that that had alarmed her. It was the first time that she had thought of him as an old man. In short, she divulged to me only the stage directions of that particular drama. She didn't feel comfortable in that house that she barely knew, or even with her own father! And, I ask the prosecutor, had she told anything *to them?*

Nothing other than the tip of the iceberg. But, to be precise, did she know more about it?

In my opinion? . . . Muratore wasn't stupid. He wasn't the kind of guy to reveal everything just like that . . . A tough nut to crack.

Did I know why he had been pushed aside by Bargeco?

Retirement, I thought.

No. That was his version. Was I unaware that he was, in a way, the recruiter for emergency manpower?

Certainly I was aware of that. It had been said a few minutes ago. It had been known since the suicide!

Not to mention the "fuckable flesh" . . . he apologized, that was the phrase that had been used.

Supposing that I had had an interview with Muratore on the construction site—which wasn't the case!—could the tribunal imagine that Muratore was stupid enough to tell me about that?

Muratore selected beauties, male or female. He examined them as if at a country fair. He of course took advantage of them himself. After which, he pimped them to the workers on the construction site, first choice given according to seniority.

Of course it's appalling . . .

There was a pause. The presiding judge had difficulty containing his growing anger. I thought about changing gears and bringing into the conversation the large special report which *République-Matin* had published at a time when construction was already very controversial. There also, in that account, you had to wonder if this report should be considered more idealistic than ignorant or the opposite.

And so, what did I want to say about that?

That I wasn't the only one to . . . what was I getting into? I should have kept my big mouth shut. Weak spot, Stéphane, weak spot! I said again that I, at least, had written nothing, published nothing . . .

Yes . . . I did well to turn the conversation toward that! The public prosecutor was going to forget . . . The people in the court started to laugh one more time. Who said that the *République-Matin* text, rightly speaking, wasn't mine?

What?

An expert stylistician, armed with all the modern statistical methods, had looked into this newspaper and concluded in favor of a certain hypertrophy of syntactical turns of phrase that were a bit strained, which indicated definitively a pen of my caliber . . . Not to mention the ratio of the frequency of certain words to my prior works. It was altogether a serious matter . . .

I didn't ask, this time, if I were the witness or the culprit. The presiding judge said to the public prosecutor that he didn't have to report on this expert opinion, in spite of its interest, since I was not on the bench of the accused.

Despite that, I was stunned. More than anything else,

the uses to which my prose had been put placed me in jeopardy. I wondered if, after that, I would still be able to make my living as a writer.

That wasn't all. They had good reason to believe . . .

What now?

. . . good reason to believe that I had written the presidential speech . . .

Participated in writing! Obviously . . . I am the one who told them that!

. . . relative to the secrecy of the construction site, in private with him. The text advanced the idea that the painters of the Renaissance who painted frescos on the chancels of a church (this could take them ten or fifteen years) started by putting up a wall in order to work in secret. The sponsor himself didn't have the right to go see it . . .

That one, yes, but I didn't write any other speeches.

Why?

Because it was very boring work! And because they didn't want to pay me. They said that my stipend was sufficient!

It was going to be necessary to stop there, before I felt justified in sending them a bill for my interrogation!

I was crushed by this underhanded hostility.

Then, the prosecutor said that he had no more questions to pose to the witness. The lawyers for the defense hadn't bothered to interrogate me. As the presiding judge was surprised by this, one of them consented to stand and to say that, quite obviously, I hadn't seen much, for the good reason that there wasn't much to see, a lot less in any case than was asserted—a little late—by these New Innocents, or those who proclaimed themselves such. With that, I was brusquely dismissed. But the presiding judge still had a question. I was waiting for an act of treachery, but not of this type, as trivial as it was gratuitous. Did I know what had become of Miss Muratore?

I had already said that I hadn't seen her again since the suicide of her father . . . a little more than a year.

And yet she had preserved a great deal of affection for me. She hoped that I was going to carry on with my brilliant work. It's what she said, at the time of her hearings. So, why hadn't I seen her again?

I had no desire to answer. If I had answered, I would have been able to say only: because she didn't want to, because she had needed me for that exact moment, not afterwards. And that she had other dreams. Sometimes things don't work out. I must have made a little bit of a sad face admitting that. I wanted to look sad, in case she might see me live on TV and grow sad too. But trials aren't systematically filmed. When they are, they aren't broadcast live. So I couldn't speak to her this way . . . but let it be understood that I still felt a great longing to be with her, if that had been her wish. Unfortunately, in her eyes, my image had been contaminated by the horrors of Mountain R, horrors that I had at very least caught a glimpse of. I hadn't even known how to write that novel, as I wouldn't write the one on Pierre Louis Moreau de Maupertuis. Definitely, she would see me as desperate! I was beginning to doubt that I could publish other books . . . The fact that I had told her so little of the drama in which her father had played such a sinister role had obviously destroyed my chances. Stupidly enough, I had scored against my own team. This damned propensity for silence . . . I can't do anything about it. Upon her return to Boston, and her begrudging kiss at the airport, I felt all of a sudden that I was becoming her father's double, a nasty feeling that made my stomach drop, like when a ship yaws in a heavy sea. I felt as if I didn't exist. As for him, even if he hadn't yet committed suicide, it was nonetheless clear that he had been shrunken, as if by headhunters, and that in the general inventory of humanity there was suddenly lacking an item, gone without a trace, something that was neither precisely me nor Muratore, but half of each . . . She had begun to ask me, in turn, questions that were difficult and insistent—but not aggressive—concerning the white-washing of my record that I hoped would result from my trip to the Pole . . . She let me see how little she cared for such a prospect.

It was necessary to ask me why I was suddenly so pale. I passed my hand over my face and rubbed my eyes.

Wait! The presiding judge gave me a sentence to add to my meditation: "Eat fish when you're fresh." It was a so-called Laplander proverb, but I took it as crude, and probably apocryphal.

One last thing before suspending the session and finishing with my precious testimony: hadn't I been surprised, here, to hear my ex-friend called *Miss* Muratore?

No, why?

Clearly, then, I was unaware that she had gotten married, and that she'd given birth, all at once, to several children.

SELECTED DALKEY ARCHIVE PAPERBACKS

PIERRE ALBERT-BIROT, *Grabinoulor.*
YUZ ALESHKOVSKY, *Kangaroo.*
FELIPE ALFAU, *Chromos.*
  Locos.
  Sentimental Songs.
IVAN ÂNGELO, *The Celebration.*
  The Tower of Glass.
ALAN ANSEN, *Contact Highs: Selected Poems 1957-1987.*
DAVID ANTIN, *Talking.*
DJUNA BARNES, *Ladies Almanack.*
  Ryder.
JOHN BARTH, *LETTERS.*
  Sabbatical.
ANDREI BITOV, *Pushkin House.*
LOUIS PAUL BOON, *Chapel Road.*
ROGER BOYLAN, *Killoyle.*
IGNÁCIO DE LOYOLA BRANDÃO, *Zero.*
CHRISTINE BROOKE-ROSE, *Amalgamemnon.*
BRIGID BROPHY, *In Transit.*
MEREDITH BROSNAN, *Mr. Dynamite.*
GERALD L. BRUNS,
  Modern Poetry and the Idea of Language.
GABRIELLE BURTON, *Heartbreak Hotel.*
MICHEL BUTOR, *Mobile.*
  Portrait of the Artist as a Young Ape.
JULIETA CAMPOS, *The Fear of Losing Eurydice.*
ANNE CARSON, *Eros the Bittersweet.*
CAMILO JOSÉ CELA, *The Family of Pascual Duarte.*
  The Hive.
LOUIS-FERDINAND CÉLINE, *Castle to Castle.*
  London Bridge.
  North.
  Rigadoon.
HUGO CHARTERIS, *The Tide Is Right.*
JEROME CHARYN, *The Tar Baby.*
MARC CHOLODENKO, *Mordechai Schamz.*
EMILY HOLMES COLEMAN, *The Shutter of Snow.*
ROBERT COOVER, *A Night at the Movies.*
STANLEY CRAWFORD, *Some Instructions to My Wife.*
ROBERT CREELEY, *Collected Prose.*
RENÉ CREVEL, *Putting My Foot in It.*
RALPH CUSACK, *Cadenza.*
SUSAN DAITCH, *L.C.*
  Storytown.
NIGEL DENNIS, *Cards of Identity.*
PETER DIMOCK,
  A Short Rhetoric for Leaving the Family.
ARIEL DORFMAN, *Konfidenz.*
COLEMAN DOWELL, *The Houses of Children.*
  Island People.
  Too Much Flesh and Jabez.
RIKKI DUCORNET, *The Complete Butcher's Tales.*
  The Fountains of Neptune.
  The Jade Cabinet.
  Phosphor in Dreamland.
  The Stain.
WILLIAM EASTLAKE, *The Bamboo Bed.*
  Castle Keep.
  Lyric of the Circle Heart.
JEAN ECHENOZ, *Chopin's Move.*
STANLEY ELKIN, *A Bad Man.*
  Boswell: A Modern Comedy.
  Criers and Kibitzers, Kibitzers and Criers.
  The Dick Gibson Show.
  The Franchiser.

  George Mills.
  The Living End.
  The MacGuffin.
  The Magic Kingdom.
  Mrs. Ted Bliss.
  The Rabbi of Lud.
  Van Gogh's Room at Arles.
ANNIE ERNAUX, *Cleaned Out.*
LAUREN FAIRBANKS, *Muzzle Thyself.*
  Sister Carrie.
LESLIE A. FIEDLER,
  Love and Death in the American Novel.
FORD MADOX FORD, *The March of Literature.*
CARLOS FUENTES, *Terra Nostra.*
  Where the Air Is Clear.
JANICE GALLOWAY, *Foreign Parts.*
  The Trick Is to Keep Breathing.
WILLIAM H. GASS, *The Tunnel.*
  Willie Masters' Lonesome Wife.
ETIENNE GILSON, *The Arts of the Beautiful.*
  Forms and Substances in the Arts.
C. S. GISCOMBE, *Giscome Road.*
  Here.
DOUGLAS GLOVER, *Bad News of the Heart.*
KAREN ELIZABETH GORDON, *The Red Shoes.*
PATRICK GRAINVILLE, *The Cave of Heaven.*
HENRY GREEN, *Blindness.*
  Concluding.
  Doting.
  Nothing.
JIŘÍ GRUŠA, *The Questionnaire.*
JOHN HAWKES, *Whistlejacket.*
AIDAN HIGGINS, *A Bestiary.*
  Flotsam and Jetsam.
  Langrishe, Go Down.
ALDOUS HUXLEY, *Antic Hay.*
  Crome Yellow.
  Point Counter Point.
  Those Barren Leaves.
  Time Must Have a Stop.
MIKHAIL IOSSEL AND JEFF PARKER, EDS.,
  *Amerika: Contemporary Russians View the
  United States.*
GERT JONKE, *Geometric Regional Novel.*
JACQUES JOUET, *Mountain R.*
DANILO KIŠ, *Garden, Ashes.*
  A Tomb for Boris Davidovich.
TADEUSZ KONWICKI, *A Minor Apocalypse.*
  The Polish Complex.
ELAINE KRAF, *The Princess of 72nd Street.*
JIM KRUSOE, *Iceland.*
EWA KURYLUK, *Century 21.*
VIOLETTE LEDUC, *La Bâtarde.*
DEBORAH LEVY, *Billy and Girl.*
  Pillow Talk in Europe and Other Places.
JOSÉ LEZAMA LIMA, *Paradiso.*
OSMAN LINS, *Avalovara.*
  The Queen of the Prisons of Greece.
ALF MAC LOCHLAINN, *The Corpus in the Library.*
  Out of Focus.
RON LOEWINSOHN, *Magnetic Field(s).*
D. KEITH MANO, *Take Five.*
BEN MARCUS, *The Age of Wire and String.*
WALLACE MARKFIELD, *Teitlebaum's Window.*
  To an Early Grave.

FOR A FULL LIST OF PUBLICATIONS, VISIT:
www.dalkeyarchive.com